“And Burnt The Topless Towers” is a debut novel.
The author, Cliff Dix, has worked in the entertainment industry for over
forty-five years. His autobiographical reminiscences are published in
“Up the Fire Escape and Through the Kitchens”

ISBN 9781849146487

Thanks to Carl Theobald for his advice on combustion.

To Ann, for her patience while all that typing was going on!

AND BURNT THE TOPLESS TOWERS

All characters and events in this book are fictitious, and any resemblance to any real person living or dead is purely co-incidental.

Chapter 1

Afterwards they agreed it was when the Devil appeared that all the trouble started. But the problems had really begun long before that.

The show had first been advertised in June, and the dispute about it in the staff room of the Thomas Lincoln School just inside one of the leafier suburbs of the city had gone on almost till the school broke up for the long summer holidays. The school lay in one of those areas where roads called 'Avenue' threaded a sinusoidal pattern around semi detached houses with bay windows and car parking spaces on what had formerly been front gardens. These desirable properties, to quote estate agents, were on roads that joined a main trunk route around the city. On the other side of this thoroughfare ruler straight rows of small terraced houses opened directly onto the pavement, interspersed by occasional launderettes, off licences and general stores where the pervading odour was a striking mixture of cleaning fluids and curry. Once in a while the rows were broken by a new structure, with plate glass windows overlaid by giant, but fading, stuck on pictures of fresh fruit and vegetables across the entire glass surface, as if the owners were ashamed to allow passers by to look in, or feared allowing their employees at the check-outs to see out. These were the supermarkets, recently imposed on the terraces and linked in every case to a major chain who's main stores were a car's journey away.

Inside the 1970s school building the irresistible force of John Scarings' youthful enthusiasm came up against the immoveable doubt of Miss Robinson. It was not the first time that they had clashed, and Patsy Newbon wished, as she often did, that they wouldn't fight so openly, or so vehemently.

Amid the badly washed and ill assorted coffee mugs, one advising 'Keep Calm and Ask a Teacher', and the frank litter of paperwork and marking, the poster and little pile of flyers for the show lay on the staff room table between them.

"It's part of their coursework." John insisted as he opened his diary.

Miss Robinson snorted.

"We're here to make them study the text, not take them out on pleasure trips."

"Ah, here, look, I've got some of Year 10 anyway on a Friday afternoon, so we'd just need to get Mr Brewster to let the other handful of them out of geography and we could take the whole group."

"It's not even a proper production of it." Miss Robinson's sour mouth snapped, "A musical!"

She managed to make the word 'musical' sound like a disease.

John glanced at the poster. It was, he had to concede, somewhat garish. It gave the impression that the denizens of page three were being overwhelmed by hell-fire. But despite it being clearly at odds with the dry literary study of a play text that the English department under Miss Robinson favoured he stuck to his guns.

"It will engage the pupils and make them more interested in the text."

"Engage!", another snort from his head of department. She'd been in front of classes of pupils long enough to have heard, and dismissed, a long succession of buzz-words, and was a shrewd enough practitioner to understand that most of them had no relevance to her style of teaching and to recognise them as fashionable verbiage purely designed to make the most mundane statement sound important. She was, however, also aware that her style was old fashioned and that the modern trends were gradually ousting her and her peers. She looked forward, in a way, to retirement, and her reluctance was, she realised, partly due to a wish for an easy last couple of years.

She knew that shepherding a school party around in the city centre, boarding buses, seating them in an auditorium, returning them to the school afterwards, arranging for parents to collect those who lived a distance away, and counting, recounting, and counting again, because someone would be certain to wander off, would be wearing and hard on her ageing nerves. John's use of the word 'handful', though he had referred to a quantity, had resonated with her perception of teenage pupils on the move.

That this should be so that the pupils could watch a musical version of one of the set texts, and modern musical at that, did not appeal to her at all.

"Anyway" she snapped, "there's no budget for it, so it's pointless discussing it."

'There,' she thought 'that's stopped him in his tracks.'

"I've thought of that. If we do a block booking we get a discount. Lovells the coach hire firm will do us a deal because it's very local and they happen to be able to fit it in with their existing bookings. I asked them. so what we save on the tickets will more than cover the buses which will still let us charge the pupils less than the full theatre ticket price."

"You'll never get them all to pay, and you'll be left with spare tickets so we'll lose money. Money the department hasn't got."

"I promise you they'll all come, and anyway the Drama

department say they'll take up any slack."

He shouldn't really have mentioned the Drama department. Miss Robinson had little time for namby pamby subjects. She believed in the three 'Rs', reading 'riting and 'rithmetic, seeing most of the rest of the modern curriculum as soft option fads that would be of little of no use in the real world.

"You had no business talking to them before I had decided whether I would allow this jaunt!"

Before John could reply the staffroom door crashed open and their private spat was invaded by a whirlwind of a man clutching an untidy pile of paper which he dumped unceremoniously on the table on top of the poster.

"Talking about this theatre trip then?" the newcomer queried brightly.

Small, bouncy, with a cruel wit and an irrepressible zest for life and all its challenges, Nick Arthur was the head of the Drama department. The pupils referred to him as 'Tigger', a nickname that had been taken up by some of the staff too in private, and he had an extraordinarily thick skin which stood him in good stead in most of his dealings with the head of English.

"This 'theatre trip' as you put it will not be happening" Miss Robinson stated flatly.

"Why not?" queried 'Tigger, "Something good on tele that night?"

"Miss Robinson doesn't feel that a musical version would be a good experience for the children." explained John.

"Oh come on. Just because you can remember the first night of the original...."

"I'll thank you not to be insulting..."

".......Royal Shakespeare Company's last production." Tigger finished cleverly wriggling out of blame for the trap that he had arranged for Miss Robinson.

The war of words and opinions raged on. No one included Patsy in the discussion. They never did. And although her ideas were very much in line with the two male teachers it would not have occurred to her to put her view forward. If the truth were to be told she was a shy, nervous, almost mousey young woman. She was easily browbeaten by the elder head of department, overawed by the boisterous staff around her and the subject of considerable bad behaviour and disobedience by the pupils she taught.

Her evenings were spent in welcome escape from the rigours of the school in her small flat. She rarely went out, being too reticent to join new groups of people. Perhaps if John had asked her she might, she thought. But like most of the staff he seemed to hardly notice her. She was quite pretty, but a plain dresser, choosing clothes in shades of beige that belied her youth. She did hope that the trip would go ahead. She quite enjoyed the very occasional visits that she made to the theatre, and this chance to see a major touring production was very tempting. Moreover if the school party went ahead as John was advocating she would have the chance to attend something as part of a group, rather than on her own.

People always seemed to notice her if she was alone. Audiences were usually made up of couples, and her solitary attendances seemed to make her conspicuous, a thing she dreaded.

Her diffidence had afflicted her since childhood. She was the only child of a family who's successful engineering business covered several acres, and employed over a hundred men. And there was the start of the problem. For her father, Arthur

Newbon, had, naturally it seemed to him, wanted a son to pass his empire to. Patsy's childhood had, therefore, been a succession of attempts to force her into what her father saw as suitable activities. Sports, preferably highly active ones, featured high on Arthur's preferred menu. Academically she was pressured to the sciences and there had been some attempt to push her towards an engineering degree. She was capable of this. In fact her background had given her a better grasp of practical science and engineering than her school staffroom colleagues in the science departments. But capability and interest are not the same, and as soon as the opportunity arose to move towards the arts she had seized it with both hands, studying at a university as far from the parental engineering firm as she could manage, before taking this teaching post some hundred miles from her family home for lack of any alternative career path.

She was roused from her thoughts now by a fierce outburst from Miss Robinson. She had finally had to concede to the others demands, and was going down fighting by laying out areas of responsibility.

It would be they, she was insisting, who would deal with the distribution of forms for parents to fill in, with the 'risk assessment', with collecting, or arranging for the school office to collect, the money. It would be they who would have to square the arrangements with the head and with other departments. They should deal with the parents who didn't want to pay up. Most of all, before the trip, and during it, it should be they who dealt with bus-loads of stroppy teenagers outside the controlled environs of the school.

When the letter went out to the parents after the summer holidays, in September, the 'stroppy teenagers' reacted in mixed ways. Some simply lost, or failed to hand over, the letter, and these few caused the bulk of the organisational problems. There were those who didn't want to go, and were sent by enthusiastic parents and those who wanted to go and had to persuade their parents

"I really need to go, Mum" pleaded fifteen year old Gemma Barrents.

Actually Gemma had no real interest in the show. She had a schoolgirl crush on John Scarings, and was on the look out for any opportunity to spend more than just the timetabled classroom hours in his presence.

The minutes before any class with him would find her carefully brushing her long dark hair, touching up whatever make-up she had managed to get away with wearing that day, and pulling the waistband of her school skirt up a bit to reveal more of her legs.

She was a pretty teenager.

Such crushes were not entirely unusual. Many students files and notebooks sported biroed graffiti that incorporated initials of the temporarily fanciable member of staff. Gemma had carried this torch for some time now however. Long enough for it to be noticed by not only John Scarings himself, but also several other members of staff. Sensitive to the situation, and the possibility of misinterpretation by others he was a great pains to keep his dealings with Gemma scrupulously fair and very above board.

For her part the girl put extra effort into her English work for Mr Scarings, and was a little disappointed whenever her marks, though better than her general grades would have suggested, never soared to any giddy heights.

"I really tried." she had remonstrated on one occasion when the grade he gave her for an essay wasn't what she had hoped. John had remained steadfastly resistant to her appeal.

Now she turned her powers of persuasion on her mother over

the matter of the theatre trip.

Her mother, a single mum who'd been not a great deal older than Gemma was now when she had had her, failed to see the importance of a theatre trip, but would bow to pressure eventually after her daughter had run the full gamut of pleading, shouting and sulking. Thus Gemma was able to come in to school with the signed form and the payment, in cash, before the due date.

She tried, of course, to hand the slightly dog-eared envelope over to John Scarings, and was a little cast down at being sent to the school secretaries with it.

In the school office her form joined a growing pile of others. This was the pile of forms that John and 'Tigger' would use to calculate the number of buses required. They photocopied the various class registers and marked those pupils who had returned the forms. Just as expected there were several gaps.

"Paula Morley!" Tigger snorted during one of their totalling up sessions. 'Well she's no loss to the audience. She wouldn't understand it if she did go.'

John would usually have objected to this sort of denigration of a pupil, but he was willing to overlook it in the case of Paula Morley. Tiny of stature, you could be forgiven for using the expression 'emaciated', Paula was possibly the least academic of all the pupils in the school. Her attention span was apparently very short, and her tiny frame was regularly overlooked or ignored during lessons, most of which she spent staring out of the window from a back corner seat.

It was something of a surprise to them to receive Paula's form and payment the very next day.

At the Imperial Theatre Paula Morley's aunt tutted, and worked her vacuum cleaner a little harder in that part of the auditorium down by the orchestra pit rail where a daily layer of brownish dust gathered. She was fifty-eight and overweight. The extra effort was a nuisance.

She'd commented on this dust when she'd first been moved to this section of the auditorium about ten years ago. No-one seemed interested, and now it was just a fact of life. Irritating, but of little concern.

Perhaps it was her imagination, or was it getting worse, she thought. She attacked the orchestra pit drapes with the nozzle attachment for a few moments, then turned the machine off and dragged it back to the cleaners' room where she knew the kettle would be boiling.

A couple of specks of the brownish dust floated down from the Imperial's heights to start the day's deposit on the newly cleaned carpet.

Just over a hundred miles North of the Imperial, in a similar theatre in Scotland, the show's touring electrician spent part of the morning testing the lighting rig. He vaguely noticed that the second moving head from the stage on the prompt side seemed to be slightly slow in responding. But as it ended in the correct position after each movement he ignored it.

He was hot. He'd been working on this show for nearly three months, since it started the tour, and expected to be with it for at least another three. Beyond that the future was vague. Late autumn theatre bookings were the preserve of panto and managements had not been keen on this show for the December period. It was booked to run in the new year, but Christmas looked likely to be a period of what the industry calls 'resting' for all those involved. Now a hundred and fifty performances into the run Alistair was filled with the ennui that comes with a long run. A Christmas of leisure, for once, had attractions he had decided. He shut down the control and went off to get some lunch before the matinee.

Backstage in the gents chorus dressing room a minor cast member called Sandy James decided that he'd got indigestion again, took an antacid tablet, and swayed slightly as he recovered his balance. These dizzy spells were nearly as much a nuisance as his stomach.

Chapter 2

Megan and Tom were fighting again. Another Sunday, another row. It didn't really matter what it was about, it had now become a regular ritual. Not every weekend, because Megan only came home to their flat in North London on weekends when the show was staying at a venue for another week. Generally this meant three or perhaps four consecutive weekends when she would return, in the early hours of Sunday morning, from whatever city the show was playing, then there would be a fortnight's absence as the company got out from one venue, travelled and arrived at a new theatre, a new town.

In many ways Megan had now come to look forward to changeover weekends and the interest of a new venue, even those that she knew well from previous tours. She was a twenty-six year old of the type that used to be called a bubbly blonde. Short, slightly plump, and with a keen mind and happy sense of humour. She was exceptionally good at her job. At new venues on the tour she looked forward to the novelty of a new resident crew, with all its highlights, foibles and weaknesses to be explored and discovered. And the blessed relief of no fighting with Tom.

The Sunday routine seemed to be vicious circle that no amount of good intentions could break.

Megan would get up late, following her overnight drive from wherever it might be. Breakfast might turn out to be Sunday lunch if she was very late. To be fair Tom did turn his hand to cooking on her one day flying visits, but there was something odd about rising from an abbreviated sleep to be confronted with a roast dinner. She supposed she could have commented on this, but it would have been just one more thing to stir the war of sniping words that had become their default position.

None the less the social niceties would probably see them

through to early afternoon. Megan would recount tales of the latest events on tour, and Tom would sit glumly listening.

Much of the problem lay with Tom, and his current period of 'resting'.

For Tom was an actor, or at least he had been. It was nearly a year now since any meaningful part had come his way, and, now in his thirties, even he was starting to accept that he was not destined for stardom.

They'd met when she was the stage manager of a small scale fringe show he was appearing in, in a woefully inadequate 'theatre' over the bar of a noisy pub. The deservedly long forgotten show had run there to audiences of a few dozen intense and arty patrons each night, with a background sound track of the pub downstairs where the clink of glasses, crash of discarded bottles being thrown away and periodic animal whoops for a goal on the big screens that continually showed sport.

Neither of them had enjoyed the experience, but they'd formed the sort of friendship, and then relationship, that led logically to sharing a flat, making it possible for both of them to retain a London base and address.

Megan's competence had led to a succession of stage management jobs which had culminated in the current 'grade A' tour as DSM.

Tom's career had dwindled, and he now spent considerably more time as a casual barman than he did treading the boards in any capacity.

It was not this that caused the arguments,, but it contributed ammunition for both sides when the fighting started. They could fight about almost anything, but more and more they both realised that a smouldering jealousy in Tom for Megan's successful career was souring the relationship. He resented the back seat that he had to take, and became free with his criticism of her 'taking him for granted' when she arrived back from a venue.

No longer did he make allowance for the two performances she had run, followed by a late night drive, usually of several hours, to return to their home.

And the result of Tom's antagonism was that Megan made fewer journeys back to the London flat, fuelling the growing distance between them.

More often now she would stop over in the tour's digs, finding her Sunday amusement in the local cinema, or just lounging around reading the papers.

She justified it as economy. After all the petrol costs, even for her little car, which was an elderly Nissan, ate into the budget. Sustaining the flat now took a major part of her income, since the original sharing of costs had shifted as a result of Tom's 'resting'. But the truth was that there was an ever decreasing desire to go home. She knew that an argument was almost inevitable. She knew that Sunday would involve shouting amid the tedious routine of a weeks worth of washing and repacking ready for another long drive back to the tour venue. She knew too that even the inevitable sexual rapprochement following the row was no longer enjoyable enough to recompense for the unpleasantness. Too often now she found herself lying below him with her mind elsewhere, probably considering the content of the most recent spat, while she waited for his movements to reach their inevitable conclusion.

For his part Tom saw her weekend absences as her making the show and the tour a priority over him. Sullenly he accepted those solitary weekends, but the resentment grew, making the fights more likely. He too was now feeling that

Sunday afternoon sex was no longer a real compensation though he never considered missing out on the sensations once their physical activities halted their verbal attacks.

Now they were shouting at each other again.

"You don't care. You've got all your friends at the theatre and I'm stuck here on my own."

"You aren't on your own. You're leaning on a bar counter yapping to the punters."

"I'm working."

"Well so am I."

"And don't you like us all to know it."

"I don't need all this," Megan yelled, "I've got a hundred and ninety mile drive back to some grotty digs to manage a show in order to keep a roof over your head".

So there it was, out in the open again, the running sore of their relationship.

She began flinging clothes into her case, grabbing them from the pile by the ironing board, from the drawers by the bed, even, still slightly damp, if warm, from the tumble drier.

"Where are you going?"

"Back to work where people appreciate me."

If he had grabbed her and pressed himself upon her at that moment she might have responded, and another Sunday afternoon argument might have been suppressed by their coupling. But his anger had taken control of him, and he could no more have tried to win her round at that moment than he could have apologised.

She slammed the case, fought angrily with a jammed lock that wouldn't fasten, forced it, hoisted the case and flounced out of the door.

"That's right, run away. Leave me to... wash up." he finished lamely.

The Nissan failed to start, and she sat in the driver's seat furiously turning the key until it fired, while Tom stood on the step just outside the front door. It crossed his mind to plead for her to return, but he could not bring himself to do so. Deep inside he felt that she had been unfair. At the same time he was worried that this was the worst ever outcome to any row they had had. He was suddenly dismayed and a cold fear clutched his stomach. Later he would rationalise this as righteous anger. She pushed the car into gear and swerved out of the parking space across the path of some oncoming traffic, the leading car of which flashed its lights at her angrily, and away towards the north-bound trunk road.

Tom realised this was probably the end. Turning back into the flat he tried to analyse how he felt. He was honest enough to acknowledge that he was not very upset. He was sorry that the weekend had passed without their usual sex. He was sad that they had parted on cross words, and had some concern for her driving in a temper. He was mostly worried about how the situation would affect his accommodation.

In the car Megan was puzzling over how she could oust him from the flat.

It was late September.

Chapter 3

As the curtain fell on the second performance of the show on the Saturday night following Megan and Tom's split a well oiled machine lurched into operation.

Each department of the touring show started the business of packing its equipment and loading the small fleet of articulated lorries that were queued ready outside the theatre's loading bay.

Wardrobe had a head start on all the other aspects of the show, as they'd stowed and loaded the ironing boards, washing machines, driers and maintenance equipment that accompanies any big production. Cast costumes had been packed and rolled out to the scene dock by the loading doors as they had been finished with throughout this last performance at this venue. The four wardrobe staff had only to retrieve the last costume from each dressing room, pack it and watch the skips and boxes disappear onto the first lorry before heading off to their digs. They would retrieve the garments at the next venue and be washing and ironing by Sunday afternoon.

Susie tramped round the dressing room block checking for those small items that might have got left on shelves or in the corner of work surfaces. In dressing room after dressing room she found only empty rails, waste-paper bins full of screwed up tissues, with, probably, the Saturday newspaper folded to a half completed crossword stuffed on top.

She was surprised, in dressing room eleven, to find Sandy James still there. One of the men's chorus rooms was an empty, echoing and deserted shell, like all the rest. But sat on a chair by the mirrors and surrounded by the debris and litter of a few weeks occupation by half a dozen of the cast, his luggage at his feet, was Sandy.

"Hello, are you OK?" Susie asked, slightly concerned.

Sandy seemed to drag himself back from some distant place and looked up at her. He struggled to his feet and hefted his bag with an obvious effort.

"Yes, thanks, just on my way." he said, and made for the door.

Susie looked after his retreating back as he made his way down the corridor to go down the stairs. She was suddenly aware of how old he seemed in relation to the rest of the cast. Shaking her head slightly she continued her checks of the abandoned rooms. With the casualness of youth she soon temporarily forgot the encounter. It would be several days before she called the incident to mind again and her naturally caring disposition made her watch him more carefully.

Amid metallic clangs and thumps the scenery was coming apart into its component units. Thirty foot wide sections of steel framed backings, with fitted wiring and cables flew in from the grid to be dismantled and sent out for loading. Sections of aluminium trussing, complete with the lighting they supported came down to floor level for the first time in a month and were swiftly unplugged and sent out to waiting lorries.

In the auditorium chain hoists chattered as more truss, bearing moving heads, descended from the auditorium sides and the front of the balcony. The moving heads were numbered. They were taken off the suspended trussing and packed in flight cases which were wheeled onto the loading bay. No one noticed the second moving head down from the proscenium on prompt side being banged against the rim of the flight case as it was packed. The mover was number twenty-three. They probably wouldn't have worried if they had. The 'movers' were heavy robust bits of kit. Costing well over a thousand pounds each they were designed for the rigours of the road. They were on hire to the show from a big and reputable London based hire company that specialised in major music concerts. The show was carrying forty of these. Two dozen of them were positioned front of house, that is on the audience side of the proscenium arch, at each venue. Twelve formed a row of lighting upstage, facing towards the audience and were mostly used as back-light. There were two others each side of stage on vertical truss booms largely bearing conventional, that is non moving, lanterns, as the theatre industry calls them.

The electrics department of the show was carrying two spare movers too, in case of breakdowns. These were in a flight case that had not been opened since the show began its tour.

Each 'mover' was an intense light able to pan left and right and tilt up and down. The unit also received control information that could make it fade up and down, strobe, change colour, insert a gobo, (an etched metal plate that produced a pattern in the beam) and even rotate the gobo so the pattern spun on the stage. The unit received 'instructions' from the lighting desk down a simple cable in the form of digital pulses known as a DMX signal. The show had been programmed into the desk during the first venue's get in, the so called 'production weekend', and the touring operator simply ensured that each lantern was connected to the correct dimmer and pointed in the correct place whenever the show moved. The movers were a bit more complex, as repositioning them from venue to venue sometimes changed their orientation in respect of the stage, and thus the exact pan and tilt information required for every cue in the show.

To deal with this the touring desk had a facility that allowed the operator to establish some fixed points on the new stage, usually the four corners, and let the desk adjust each individual mover's positional DMX instruction for the whole show at the press of a single button.

It had been while double checking this that the touring operator had noticed that mover number twenty-three was responding a bit slowly. The unit was controlled from and responded to digital address number three hundred and sixty-eight in the first 'universe' of five hundred and twelve DMX addresses coming from the lighting control desk.

In order to turn through a pan arc of almost a whole circle, and a tilt arc of about two thirds of a circle the mover was constructed with the lantern itself suspended in a yoke, which was able to pivot. Thus the lantern could both somersault in its yoke and be panned around by the yoke itself. Stepper motors controlled the positioning of both the 'x' and 'y' axis. It was possible to mount the mover in any orientation, and although the front of house and back-light units were hung from horizontal trussing the two on each side boom were mounted with their base-plates in a vertical position. Confusingly this meant that when programming the show in the case of these four lanterns pan became tilt and vice-versa.

Despite this the operators mostly thought of the tilt direction as that where there head pivoted in its yoke. The yoke was a hollow clamshell construction, with no solid load-bearing parts inside. Clever design reduced the weight and used the yoke's own shape to provide a rigid frame which supported the bearings that held the stubby axles that stuck out of each side of the casing of the head itself. Some concealed cabling ran in through these axles to provide power to the lamp and to operate a shutter, the colour wheel and the disc containing the gobos.

This cabling could not twist up as the tilt motion was considerably less than a full circle before the unit met its end stop and had to be returned.

The tilt stepper motor drove the axles of the head via a toothed belt that sat on a matching pulley. This allowed considerable precision in positioning the beam of light.

The clamshell yoke remained exceptionally strong so long as the two halves were aligned.

Some previous knock had dislodged these slightly, causing the slow response the operator had noticed by throwing the sprocket and belt out of true. Now this second knock had worsened the situation. No-one knew this, and it would have taken a very close examination of the unit to have seen the damage.

Dressing room four was near the stage. Not as near as the 'star' dressing rooms, but close enough to offer the stage management team the practicality of using it as both and office and pied-à-terre but also a store for the running props. For the past few weeks it had been shared between the stage management team and the touring sound and lighting technicians.

Megan and her assistant stage manager, Jane, were clearing the detritus of a month's encampment.

"The Imperial" mused Jane, climbing on a chair to reach onto the shelf above the mirrors, "That's the place with that fit ASM who fancied you when we went through last year with 'Grease'".

"He hung around all the time, I remember. And who the hell left this yoghurt pot open in this cupboard!" grumbled Megan, on her hands and knees exploring the darker recesses of the fitted storage.

"Well he can hang around me any time."

"If he's still there I'll make you a present of him." Megan promised.

"You do and you won't get him back. I'll eat him all up. Is this your phone charger?"

Jane flinched as the show relay speaker near her ear emitted an exceptionally load crash as some piece of metal-clad scenery was dismantled. She reached over and turned the volume control down. The sounds of the get-out receded, though bumps and thumps could still be heard down the corridor and the occasional heavy piece caused the timber floor to vibrate as it was dragged toward the waiting lorries.

"In any case", she added, "it's definitely you he fancies. More's the pity." and she started whistling one of the musical numbers from the show, 'Devil may care'. It was a catchy song and a version of it was currently rising rapidly up the charts.

Megan pulled herself upright, throwing a couple of discarded pages of production notes into the bin.

Did she really want to start a new 'relationship' she wondered. She'd told Jane about the last weekend's split, and suspected her of unlooked-for matchmaking. On the other hand she did remember the ASM in question, and was well aware that Jane had been a frustrated admirer of him on their last stay at The Imperial, She recalled a tall, slim and annoyingly attentive member of the house crew. His most noticeable characteristic she recalled was that through all the rigging, show running and loading and off-loading of that last show he had remained unbelievably clean and smart. He'd done his share, and perhaps more than his share, of the manual graft for the theatre, but no dirty grease stains had appeared on his shirt, no dusty knees marred his trousers. They'd commented on it. It was something of a mystery. For all the 'glamour and the glitter' show business was a filthy occupation.

What was his name? She struggled to remember.

On stage another series of metallic clangs rang out as the crew used hammers to drive out the locking pins that held the main swivelling points of the largest scenic pieces.

The set for the show incorporated several flown pieces, a permanent raised area upstage, that accommodated the on-stage part of the orchestra, which was basically a rock band and played alongside the more conventional orchestra, which was housed in the pit, and eight motorised and wheeled three dimensional steel framed trucks which were moved to different positions during the show. These ran on a false floor, laid over the host venue's stage, which was fitted with a number of swivel points. These inch and a half diameter sleeved holes were designed to take spring loaded spigot pins that protruded from the underside of the trucks.

In performance the crew positioned the truck and released the spigot so that it dropped into the socket in the stage and subsequent scenic changes were made by the motor driven wheels of the truck or trucks turning the scenic piece around this pivot point.

From time to time in the performance a spigot was withdrawn and the truck either moved to another location and it's pin inserted into another socket, or another truck came on from the wings and was locked into its position.

The choreography of the trucks was a simple established routine, and would be rehearsed during the get-in weekend and at the technical run through and dress rehearsal that took place at each venue before the show opened to the public.

During the production weekend the training of the resident crew for this and the other mechanical parts of the show fell to the production manager, a small wiry bad tempered man with a clipboard and a suit, who would leave the venue and return to his London office and the headquarters of the production company immediately after the first performance in the show's new home. Once he had gone all the running of the performances, and the checking of operation of each piece of scenery fell to the touring SM, John Mason. Unless he was in a local bar somewhere, in which case Megan naturally took over. Everyone knew about John's drinking. Everyone liked him. Everyone covered up for him.

Tonight he was sober, and assiduously watching and checking as each piece of the set came apart. He had a long and recognised career behind him and was well known throughout the touring circuit. It was probably this reputation that allowed him to retain his position on the show despite his weakness for alcohol.

As the night dragged by the stage and the grid of the theatre gradually emptied and, with a growl of low gears, lorry after lorry pulled away from the loading bay to head towards 'The Imperial', where the resident crew had already finished a rather easy get-out of a one room set of a show in a style that is dismissively known as 'drinks table behind sofa'. They had headed home for their beds to be ready for tomorrow's get-in.

The Imperial's night watchman, Stan, finished saying 'good-nights', locked the stage door behind the last departing member of staff, and went and settled himself in his favourite 'A' row seat. The old building's silence was broken only by the occasional unexplained creaks that all empty theatres are prone to, and the distant, almost inaudible, gentle hum of heating plant.

Stan was well past retirement age, and his hearing was failing. He heard none of the quiet sounds. But as so often in the past he could see a faint haze, almost a twinkle, as dust fell slowly past a night-time working light over the prompt side end of the orchestra pit.

Chapter 4

It rained. It rained all night on cursing lorry drivers ploughing through motorway spray and the distorted smear of oncoming headlights as the scattered convoy of trucks sped from the last theatre to The Imperial.

It rained on Ben Brinton, The Imperial's ASM who'd been the subject of Megan and Jane's conversation, as he walked to the theatre after he parked his car in the multi storey car park on Sunday morning. He'd left his bed-sit flat on the outskirts of the city about half an hour earlier. He lived in an area largely made up of formerly grand houses, now divided into flats and bed-sits for students. Ben's was one of these, and, though cheap, suffered from the penalty of noise and commotion at all hours of the night from the other local residents. Last night had been one such night, and Ben was weary from lack of sleep. None the less he was smart and tidy as usual. If his hair was still damp from the early morning shower the rain disguised this clue to rather hasty morning preparations.

It rained on Charlie Parnell, The Imperials's technical director, on his way in to work. Charlie too had had a short night's rest, though in his case this was due to his conscientious checking of the theatre after the previous show's get out. His own house was in a quiet suburban cul-de-sac, undisturbed by neighbours. In fact Charlie's own nocturnal comings and goings were more likely to disturb the street than otherwise.

It rained on the theatre's loading bay, making the get-in of the show a slippery, and at times dangerous, struggle for The Imperial's crew.

Charlie was a hugely experienced theatre technician. He had worked his way up through the whole range of theatre styles and sizes, from the lowliest stage-hand via lighting and sound jobs to his present post in charge of all the technical aspects of the huge theatre.

His realm now included all the various stage departments. He was in charge of the chief electrician, the stage manager and the maintenance department. He was also effectively the house engineer and probably knew more about The Imperial's hidden nooks and crannies and it's mechanical and electrical workings than anyone.

He could have run his position entirely as a pen pusher, but he was very much a 'hands on' technician. It was just as likely that he would be up a ladder focussing some lantern or other as that he would be behind his desk. This morning he would be with the rest of the crew lugging the show into the building from the lorries.

Last night one of his final acts as he left the theatre from the stage door had been to head towards the main road and look at the front of the building to make sure that the new show's advertising had been put in place. It had. Huge versions of the poster that John Scarings had thought 'garish' several months ago now adorned the ornate, hundred year old, frontage, with the scantily clad publicity images blown up to twice life size. Vivid red lettering announced the arrival, on its pre West End tour, of the rock musical "Faustus!". Smaller teaser posters reminded the public of the hit successes from the show, already being played regularly on radio stations and re-recorded and issued by a smattering of major name artists who knew a good song when they heard one and wanted to cash in.

You could find, and download, both original cast, and cover versions of several of the best known songs on a multitude of sites on the internet.

The Thomas Lincoln School had been lucky to have booked early and to have got a concessionary rate. Following the success of the show's musical numbers tickets were now at something of a premium and becoming hard to get. The Imperial was to run "Faustus!" for four weeks, and the month was as near to a sell out as you could ever hope for.

It was very difficult for any theatre to be one hundred percent full. Many customers have specific preferences, some wishing to sit at the end of rows, some wanting a central view of the stage. Although the box office, and the program that ran the on-line booking service, adopted a policy of concealing the exact situation of advance sold seats from any customer wanting to purchase seats, with a view to reducing the number of gaps that might appear in any row, there were bound to be occasional spaces. If a customer booked a party of 12 onto one end of a fifteen seat row, and another customer wished to book a pair of seats at the other end of the same row the box office could easily be stuck with a single seat mid-way along the row that no customer would be likely to want. In many ways Patsy Newbon's occasional solo theatre visits were a godsend to a harassed box office manager, though she did not know it, allowing him to fill at least one of the gaps that inevitably appeared.

Occasionally, as with a show in demand, such as "Faustus!" had turned out to be, families might find themselves split onto seats in front of and behind each other in order to see a show at all. Always a block booking, such as the school had made, or as was sometimes done by coach companies arranging 'theatre evenings' were both a blessing, as the box office could fit the requested seats into odd shaped patterns on the plan provided they sold adjacent places, or a curse, where the demanded quantity produced a single seat spare once the booking was made.

Party bookings were additionally aggravating to the theatre when organisers tried to increase, or decrease numbers after they had booked.

Such alterations were not encouraged, and the house exercised a rule that it would only refund if another customer could be found to take returned tickets.

In the case of "Faustus!" there would be no problem disposing of returned seats, but the difficulty for the next four weeks was exactly the reverse.

At the box office they were being confronted by annoyed patrons who had left it too late to book and were now being turned away. Chief among these were members of the theatre's supporters club, who paid an annual subscription, had a monthly newsletter and were allowed to book early at a slightly concessionary rate, before booking opened to the public. Now, having left it too late, several were to be found each day at the sales window berating the hapless staff.

"I belong to your supporters club!"

"Yes sir."

"I should get preferential treatment."

"Yes sir, you do get a concessionary rate for early booking, and information before the general public."

"You should be able to offer us tickets, otherwise there's no point in belonging to your club!"

"Sorry sir. It is a very popular show."

"That's why I want to see it."

The conversations turned in pointless circles.

The box office faced the central doors of the marble floored foyer entrance in the centre of the theatre's frontage. Smaller side doors led from the street into the same foyer area and signs outside attempted to encourage audience members to use the door nearest to the part of the auditorium they had booked for. Each of the side doors had been fitted in recent years with wheelchair ramps, which partially blocked the pavement outside, but the main central doors had retained the wide stairs and stubby sweeping bannisters that had been part of the original design.

Inside the foyer successive modifications had added lifts and some commercial counters for sweets and programmes, but the imposing curving staircases that bracketed the box office and led to the upper parts of the house still dominated the space. Under them, aside from the structure of the box office, were doorways that led to a corridor running the entire circumference of the stalls and giving access to the stalls seating by six sets of double doors, evenly spaced around the auditorium perimeter with thick, rich, curtains on the inside that were to keep the corridor light out of the auditorium, and to reduce any noise leakage from disturbing the show.

The general layout was repeated on the next floor, the dress circle, although the staircases that led from this level to the upper circle were smaller and slightly less grandiose.

Where both the dress circle and upper circle differed from the stalls was in having narrower perimeter corridors and less access to the foyer. This was because, just like the stalls, the spaces not occupied by the auditorium at those levels were pressed into use as bars and, especially at upper circle level, offices.

To allow for escape routes the architect had incorporated a pair of staircases leading from each of the upper levels to the street. These stairs were rather plain brick and concrete affairs which spiralled via a series of short straight flights from whichever level to the ground. On the prompt side the dress and upper circle stairways arrived at street level side by side as two blank pairs of panic doors opening into the side street that also served the loading and stage doors.

On the OP side of the building adjacent properties forced these escape routes to turn at ground level and join together in a rather unprepossessing tunnel like passage that led out to the front of the theatre.

Inside the auditorium the theatre's ornate Victorian style dominated.

Actually The Imperial's opening had taken place in the early twentieth century, just after Victoria's reign was over, but the opulent style of décor was still in vogue.

The curved dress and upper circle balcony fronts boasted mock supporting brackets and scroll-work of great intricacy that led around to the point nearest the stage where at each level and on each side a single box appeared to form the junction between the circles and the pillars that delineated the sides of the proscenium arch.

These boxes were rarely used now, as the area around them was frequently cluttered by modern lighting and sound equipment. This would be the case for "Faustus!" but demand meant that even seats with slightly restricted views would be sold.

Technical clutter also largely obscured the ornate circle frontages with each carrying a bar full of lanterns, cables and a shelf that had been fitted to prevent stray items from falling down onto the stalls seating below.

Despite these, frankly ugly, alterations The Imperial was known as one of the country's greatest theatres and was much visited by members of the public interested in historic venues.

The proscenium arch itself soared above the stage to join, or to seem to join, the auditorium ceiling where the main chandelier hung from an oval moulded boss over the stalls. The boss was supported, or gave the illusion of being, by a flight of cherubs entangled in trailing vines. In most theatres these would have been painted onto a flat plasterwork ceiling. At The Imperial the vines and the cherubs were three dimensional moulded plaster sculptures, each individually hand finished, in situ, by the builders over a hundred years earlier.

The proscenium wall formed a vertical break right through the building, dividing the opulence of front of house from the plain and rather tatty brickwork of backstage. where, although certain dressing rooms were comfortably decorated, the passages and walls of the working areas were mostly painted brick.

It was into this working world that Charlie, and, moments later, Ben entered on the Sunday morning.

They came in through the stage door which was in a narrow and easily overlooked recess in the wall that ran along the side street on prompt side. Most passing members of the public failed to register the stage door. Charlie and Ben turned left and passed the stage door keeper's tiny glass fronted box to be swallowed by the maze of corridors that led to dressing rooms, the stage and the hidden backstage stores and workshops, electrical equipment rooms, plant rooms, wardrobe and scene dock.

Ben made for the stage and, arriving in the prompt corner, reached over the stage manager's desk to press one of the large red buttons on the panel labelled 'Safety Curtain'. There was a click of a relay, and a moment's pause as the electric motor took up the slack in the system, then the safety curtain began to rise from its overnight position.

It was colloquially known as the 'iron', though it was no

longer a solid sheet of steel as had at one time been the case. Instead it consisted of a rigid metal framework fitting between a pair of tracks bolted to the sides of the proscenium arch. It was covered in flame resistant boards bolted together to produce a single solid panel that fitted the width and height of the arch. When lowered to the stage the iron provided a fireproof seal between the public in the auditorium and the stage. It was always left 'in' overnight. It was always, due to regulations, lowered and raised at some point, usually the interval, during every performance. These controlled raising and lowerings were achieved by the powerful electric motor controlled by the panel Ben had just used.

The iron could also be dropped in, to seal the proscenium in an emergency, by means of any one of several releases in different parts of the stage. These were arranged to free the brake and allow the considerable weight of the safety curtain to fall, with the electric motor driven steel hauling wires spinning the winch drum behind them, to within a few feet of the stage floor. At this point a pair of pneumatic rams or pistons cushioned the iron's descent and lowered it on the last part of its travel slowly, to an accompanying hiss of released air. This controlled descent over the last few feet was done to allow anyone, or anything, trapped below the iron to escape or be pulled free.

As the iron began its slow ascent on this morning Ben stepped out onto stage from below the overhang of fly-floor high above the prompt side wing and shouted up,

'Pull the ad-rag out Tim!'

The flyman was already on his way and the only answer Ben got was the slam of a door.

The Imperial, like many theatres, gained a small revenue by displaying the advertising for a number of local companies painted on a cloth, not unlike a small backcloth, which was shown to the audience as they came in, during the interval and after the show.

In most venues this 'ad-rag' was flown between the safety curtain and the main front of house tabs, or curtains. Here it was suspended from a batten which was flown immediately downstage, on the audience side, of the iron. All theatre flying pieces are suspended from a grid that extends from the proscenium arch to the back wall of the stage and from one side of the stage to the other. This grid holds numerous pulleys and provides a sort of bed for all the ropes and wires associated with the lifting of scenery and lighting above the stage.

The Imperial's position for the ad-rag placed this outside the grid area, so it had it's own set of lines running back to a timber platform next to the proscenium wall in the extreme corner of the auditorium roof high above the decorative plasterwork. The hemp lines came back to a hand operated winch drum which was used to raise and lower the advertisements. Access to this platform was from the fly-floor, itself some twenty-five feet above the stage, up a vertical ladder and through a heavy hatchway set in the wall. Regulations did not permit the proscenium wall to have a gap through it, so the hatchway was sealed by a double skinned door that was spring loaded to be shut. At least twice for each performance the flyman had to climb the ladder and force his way through this low doorway against the auto-closing spring, wind the advert cloth's winch, and then return.

It was an unpopular task.

In the gloom of the roof one could look down at the upper surface of the plasterwork, hidden only by the criss-crossing lines, cables and occasional catwalks. Some of these cables fed stage lighting positioned around the auditorium, some fed the house-lights.

The lines were mostly to lower specific light fittings to the auditorium floor for cleaning or lamp replacement. The heaviest line, a steel cable as thick as a man's thumb, supported the main chandelier. It was old and in several places a single strand of steel wire protruded as a palm slicing trap for the unwary. But the line had been chosen to be many times stronger than even the chandelier required, and it would continue to support the weight for many years to come. In any case the mass of sparkling glass was secured when in its position by a couple of additional chains that were shackled to fixed rings in the roof.

At one point in the gloom however the ad-rag hauling line crossed the chandelier's steel line. For several years now the point at which they crossed, and touched, happened to coincide with one of the sharp jags of steel sticking out of the steel.

Several times daily the ad-rag's ropes dragged over this point. There was no fear of them wearing through. Like the chandelier steel the ropes on the advertising cloth were over specified and would last for many years, and were, in any case, replaced at fairly regular intervals.

Tim climbed the ladder, with that odd sensation caused by the wall on his left staying still, while to his right the iron was rising on it's motorised winch just a couple of feet away from him. If he reached out and grabbed one horizontal members of the network of angle iron across its back he could have had a lift up to the access hatch. He resisted the temptation and climbed through to the auditorium side of the wall.

As the flyman flew the ad-rag out now the rope ran across the sharp steel wire and a tiny flurry of dust formed of rope particles drifted down.

The point of contact was directly above the corner of the

orchestra pit.

Finished winching Tim paused for a moment and glanced down at the top of the roof. You could follow the shapes of the decoration in the bumps and hollows of the upper side of the plasterwork, though the thickness of the material smoothed the outlines so you needed to know the roof pretty well to discern which dip was what cherub.

Peering over the edge of the platform Tim could look vertically down on the ornamental pillars that made up the side of the arch. Unusually these did not join the ceiling and any impression that an audience had that they were great structural members holding the roof over their heads was entirely illusion. They were nothing more than hollow tubes, like giant kitchen roll inners, and about as substantial.

Tim had once shone his torch down the pillars, and despite the filth of a hundred years you could see rough sawn timber formers holding what seemed to be chicken wire covered in a papier-mâché coating, supporting the outer moulded plasterwork.

Had he shone his torch down the empty cavity behind the imposing pillars on prompt side today, just after winching the ad-rag out, he might have caught a glimpse of dust motes from the ropes drifting down into the depths of the fake column.

As it was he was summoned back to his post on the fly-floor by a shout, which he heard through the plaster of the auditorium ceiling, rather than through the more substantial doorway between him and the ladder.

The get-in for "Faustus!" was under way.

The lorries which had travelled overnight were parked in a queue, nose to tail along the side street. The tour was by now routine, and the drivers had jockeyed themselves into the right order for off-loading.

It would be a miserable get-in with the rain continuing to fall creating a sodden crew struggling with the large scenic pieces and the heavier flight cases of equipment in the gap between the rear ramp of the lorry and the loading doors of the venue. Here every piece of the show had to turn through a right angle across the wide pavement and be manoeuvred up the slight bump that formed the edge of the scene dock before it could be wheeled or carried to the stage.

As the morning wore on the stage itself, and then the show's false floor became slippery with the continual traffic of wet shoes.

The resident crew was equalled in size by the touring crew, although many of these would not stay once the show was running. The touring crew identified the positions, long ago agreed, for various parts of the set and of the lighting and sound equipment, to hang, and with the locals fixed chain hoists, dead-lines and flown scenery to positions all over the stage and out into the auditorium. Once equipment was in place the vast spaghetti of power, audio and control cables emerged and was plugged in before the various parts were lifted into the air.

"Faustus!" carried a considerable amount of sound equipment as befitted its 'rock-musical' style, and by mid afternoon line array speakers would dangle alongside the truss with the moving heads on, close to the proscenium arch columns each side. The sound mixing position at the rear of the stalls lost the venue a couple of dozen seats, but the popular draw of what was shaping up to be one of the best shows of the year, with musical numbers now familiar from being regularly heard on the radio, might have off-set the management's irritation at this. However there was a feeling in the theatre offices that they could have sold those seats if the sound desk hadn't been there.

Across about three quarters of the rear of the stage a raised platform was erected that would ultimately become the on-stage band's rostrum. "Faustus!" had both a conventional orchestra in the pit and a live rock band on-stage. There were video screens in both locations so that the show conductor, in the pit, could be seen by all the musicians. Repeater screens were rigged along the front of the dress circle where they could easily be seen by the cast.

During the get-in weekend the sound department annoyed all the others by testing amps and speakers with a variety of noises and music. Alistair and the lighting department annoyed all the others by blacking out chunks of the stage and building to test and focus lanterns, and the scenic department annoyed all the others by repeatedly moving motorised trucks to different positions that were invariably in the way.

This was perfectly normal, and out of the seeming chaos a well ordered and rehearsed routine gradually emerged,

Megan had had a quick look at the prompt corner before escaping the worst of the commotion in the sanctuary of the stage management dressing room. The prompt corner was typical of theatres of this type, a timber built desk, more of a shelf really, bracketed to the upstage side of the proscenium arch brickwork just clear of the strainer wires that kept the edges of the flown front of house tabs from billowing.

A conventional timber framed permanent black masking flat each side of the stage prevented the audience from seeing into the wings, but on the prompt side a piece of black gauze had been inserted into the material of this flat to allow the stage manager to see out onto the action. Like net curtains at a window this was almost opaque to the audience during normal performance.

"Faustus!" however would not be relying on peering through a gauze panel for Megan's cueing. A row of monitors, showing various views of the stage, as well as the conductor and the on-stage group, had already appeared. As yet some of the screens were blank, and some of the cameras feeding this array were pointing at rather random angles, but once in place Megan would be able to see any part of the show that she needed to.

The technology sat incongruously with the elderly woodwork and The Imperial's prompt corner switchgear. This included an array of red and green switches for cue lights at strategic points around the stage and in each technical department, some fairly ancient headphone communication with switches, to allow Megan to talk to one, or all of the various operators, and a desk microphone on a flexible gooseneck. This microphone could be switched to allow her to talk to any or all of the backstage dressing rooms, or to speakers in the foyers and bars. The facility to make announcements front of house was repeated in the front of house manager's office.

On the wall above the desk was a large panel of switchgear. Originally this had comprised rows of round brown bakelite switches of the type once much used in houses. Each had operated some backstage function, ranging from working lights in different parts of the stage area to music stand lights in the orchestra pit and, now obsolete, fans in the prompt corner.

When first installed this panel had been regular, tidy, and labelled with engraved formica strips bearing the intended purpose of each switch.

As the years had passed many of the switches had been replaced, usually by more modern, square, metal-clad pattress mounted switches. Now the rows were uneven and adjacent switches stuck out different distances from the backing. Larger new switches had obscured the original labelling, and in any case the uses had changed, so a pastiche of sticky labels, many hand-written, joined assorted coloured tape markings on the panel to advise users of what each switch now did. Three switches were taped into the off position.

Megan was unfazed by this. This was fairly usual in old theatres.

She was slightly aggravated to find that the desk was a fraction too small to take her prompt copy fully open.

"Faustus!" had a big prompt copy, the script, and parts of the score, marked with the standby and cue for every lighting and scenic change, and with all the cast calls. It also had note of every cast member's 'blocking', (where the actor should move to on stage) which was used when understudy rehearsals were held. The prompt copy was the bible of the show.

Megan arranged for a small extra table to be set in the prompt corner. This was not for the script, or for show equipment. It was to take the inevitable can of drink, sweets, handbag and sandwiches that would accumulate in what would be her office for a working day every day for the next month. It would also take her chess set, for Megan had a habit of playing chess with a member of the resident crew by announcing the moves over the headphone communications ring and by each having a set beside them to move the pieces on.

She wasn't sure there would be a chess player on the crew at The Imperial, but there usually was. Even "Faustus!" had quite long scenes during which there was only limited technical action and the game could proceed.

She wedged the tour mascot, a soft toy of a devil given to her during the first week of the run, onto the edge of the shelf above her desk, next to a small teddy bear that had been unceremoniously attached there by means of a nail through one of its ears.

In the dressing room she selected a place for herself and unpacked the few items that would be there for the duration of the run in this venue.

"Have you heard anything from Tom?" ventured Jane.

"Oh yes." Megan told her ASM, "He sent a text yesterday."

"Oh good. That means he's sorry."

"It doesn't mean anything of the sort. He sent me a text to say that the gas bill had arrived".

There was a pause. Then Jane said,

"That ASM's still here. I saw him in a corridor earlier."

Ben, the subject of Jane's comment, was immersed in the process of receiving the show into the theatre. He'd noticed Megan's arrival, but the logistics of the fit up had kept him busy all through the morning. Would she remember him?

Chapter 5

Lunchtime saw both touring and resident crew crowding into the local pub. A heated discussion was taking place at one table. John Mason was holding forth,

"You see people think that civilisation is technology. You sit there with your mobile phones and your internet and you think you are civilised."

"Go on then. Define it another way." challenged Jane.

"Civilisation is about entertainment. You have to achieve a certain level of civilisation before you can have entertainment."

"Why?"

"There has to be time. Time to watch things, time to enjoy spectacle. Entertainment. The entertainment industry delivers on time."

"And you can't have that sort of time unless you have technology to make living possible." Alistair butted in.

"I don't think you're right about time. Look at primitive tribes, they make all sorts of elaborate head-dresses and costumes and have rituals and dances around tribal chiefs that are straight entertainment performance, and some of them are only scraping an existence." said Susie.

John waved a hand about, the contents of the glass he held in it miraculously managing not to spill.

"You're talking about religion. Different thing entirely, religion. And when I say entertainment industry I mean all of it, the theatres, the restaurants, even the taxis. You book a taxi, it turns up on time. You go to a show, it starts on time.

But you order a new road to be built and it will be finished six months late and over budget."

"I think you only get civilisation when a certain proportion of the population isn't dying violent deaths." put in Megan.

"Any specific proportion.. can we have a percentage?"

"Well if we're civilised we wake up in the morning with a pretty fair certainty that we will still be alive to go to bed in the evening."

"Why shouldn't we?"

Megan hesitated. "If you might be bombed perhaps? Or if you were a soldier."

"Ah! So when there's a war, like the First World War, or the last one, then suddenly we have stopped being civilised."

"I think you might put up a very good argument for that opinion."

"What about slavery?" Alistair asked.

"Good God, now you've shifted from defining civilisation by the existence of Berners-Lee to by the presence of the Robert E Lee!" said John

"I think," said Charlie, "that you're right about time and proper civilisation is going back to work on time without having to be hassled."

And they laughed, and gathered up their coats, drained their glasses and, with the locals shouting good-bye to the bar staff, headed back to the theatre.

"My name is Charlie." muttered one of The Imperial's crew

as the walked up the street.

"What?" asked Megan.

"I took them away from all that, and now they work for me. My name is Charlie." the stage-hand quoted to her, grinning to take the sting from the implicit grumble. "We're all 'Charlie's Angels', and don't he boss us around."

Megan wasn't old enough for the quote to register too much with her, but she recognised the fondness with which it was delivered.

The last lorry to be unloaded at The Imperial had had to wait on the main road outside the front of house entrance for space at the loading doors.

The theatre frontage was on South Parade, a wide thoroughfare that swept through the city centre and was lined with major stores. The stage door, loading bay and exits from the prompt side of the auditorium were in the side street off this main road, called Wellington Street. It was quite a tight turn from South Parade into Wellington Street for an articulated lorry.

On this Sunday the driver had been lucky and had managed to pull up on the building's frontage in the lay-by that ran the entire width of the theatre and was usually earmarked for buses and coaches delivering and collecting audiences. There were no buses that day, with the venue 'dark', the theatre term for there not being a performance.

Once he was told he could move on to the loading doors he pulled out of the lay-by, swung out past the half way point in the road and neatly turned the truck down Wellington Street. The wide pavements there could really have been used to some advantage to take some of the lorry's width while it was being off-loaded, but the lamp-posts prevented this, so the driver tucked the near side wheels as tightly in to the curb as he could and left it at that.

Fortunately Wellington Street was a little used one-way street and this parking left just enough room for the occasional vehicle to squeeze past.

The crew turned its attentions to this latest, and last truckload.

Up in the building's roof spaces ever increasing quantities of rigging lines and straps had been installed to suspend speakers and lighting over the auditorium.

Truss with moving heads attached had risen on chain hoists to its appointed positions near the side boxes. Head number twenty-three was back in its usual place in relation to the rest of the show. Still no-one had noticed anything amiss.

Tim had had to venture out into the roof void near the ad-rag hauling lines several times during the day, and the space was now festooned with a cats cradle of supporting lines. It had become fairly difficult to see out past the working platform to where the ad-rag's lines crossed the chandelier's suspension.

On the level below Charlie Parnell had his office, and could come out onto a small balcony, almost a private box, squeezed between the false pillars of the proscenium arch and the side of the first of the upper circle level public boxes. It was a location that normally enabled him to observe both the show and the audience unseen. His views would be partly restricted for the next month or so as a swathe of multicore cable, feeding the prompt side PA and the movers on the truss just above his head had been led down the building's plasterwork on a line central to his eyrie. Head number twenty-three was just above him as he stood on this extension to his office.

On the other side of the city a man called Dan stood in the window of his house and looked out across the road in the same way that Charlie was looking across the auditorium with a similar proprietorial feeling of satisfaction.

On waste ground opposite stood his most prized possession, a seven and a half ton van. More of a small lorry, it represented a major investment, and the first step up a ladder that Dan fervently hoped would lead eventually to a fleet of delivery vehicles. For the moment he was an owner operator, and worked long and hard days, and sometimes nights, to keep up the payments on the finance for the truck. It was unusual for him to be at home, even on a Sunday, but a chance combination of local bookings and his wife's birthday saw him there that day.

At his feet was his son, Simon, a lively four, nearly five year old. He was pushing a toy lorry around the carpet, making loud engine noises. Given his father's enthusiasm for his fledgeling business it was hardly surprising that the youngster had developed a strong interest in lorries and trucks. With all the small child's innate ability to absorb detail he could already identify the make and model of a score of different commercial vehicles.

Dan was concerned though. His pretty wife had just announced that she had got to go to her parents home in Scotland for a couple of days in a week's time. It wouldn't be possible for her to take Simon with her, as the trip was to make arrangements for the care of her father who was badly afflicted with dementia. She would be leaving late on Thursday afternoon, and she'd be back during Saturday. Dan would have to look after Simon for the day while Alison was away, but he couldn't cancel the delivery bookings that he had for the day.

"He'll have to come in the cab with you" said Alison.
Dan knew she was right, but he worried about Simon

spending a whole day spent cooped up in the cab of a lorry while his father loaded and off-loaded at a succession of addresses.

"Can't anyone baby-sit?"

"Oh come on," Alison responded, "You know he only likes being with Dawn, and she's on holiday. And before you start, we can't afford to pay someone. You'd end up losing money on the day's work."

Dan shrugged.

"Anyway," Alison went on, "he'll love it. He's more obsessed with that lorry than you are."

The conversation was interrupted by more engine revving noises from their son on the floor at their feet, with, this time, the addition of screeching brakes and an explosive 'crash' sound at the end, as the toy truck was hurled violently across the carpet to collide with the table leg and fall on its side.

"Don't chip my table!"

"Don't break it!"

came from the two parents simultaneously.

They looked at each other for a moment, then laughed. Alison hugged her husband.

"Well," she said, "that just about sums up the priorities."

Dan looked back at his truck outside. It looked shinier than usual in the drizzling rain.

"Dan's Van", suggested Alison.
"I want to call the company something that sounds more

important", he told her.

"I know," she said, "But I think you need to grow before you can call yourself 'Intergalactic Trucking'!"

Simon crawled across the room pushing the toy in a series of short journeys, punctuated by air brake hissing at each stop.

"Come on, lets cut your birthday cake" Dan suggested to his wife.

In a bed and breakfast not far from Dan and Alison's home, Sandy James dropped his suitcase on the floor of his room with relief, and flopped into the single armchair beside the bed. He supposed he should go out and find somewhere to have something to eat, but the effort didn't seem worthwhile. He decided to just sit quietly for a little. Maybe later he would read. Tomorrow he would make up for it by having a big breakfast. Now he just wanted to rest.

Chapter 6

Penny Abbott had come into the BBC's local radio station via the front door and been led through a series of fluorescent lit white corridors, with walls hung with huge, framed blow up photographs of the station's famous interviewees to studio 'B' where the breakfast show was being broadcast from. She hated these early morning interviews. Her co-star, Brian Marsden was already there, lounging in a swivel chair in front of a microphone. She knew he hated early mornings even more than she did.

The succession of interviews, set up by the show's publicity department in every city they played, was probably doing more for Penny's career than for Brian's. He was an already established 'name'. Penny had been a virtual unknown when she had been cast as Helen opposite his Faustus. Despite the media concentrating most of its attention on 'Devil May Care' her own numbers in the show were getting plenty of airplay, and she herself was constantly in demand for photo shoots. She felt, in the back of her mind, that she should have resented the photographic sessions as they were invariably done concentrating on her looks, and pushing towards glamour shoots within the limits of what could be used to publicise a family show.

However she'd found that she didn't care in the slightest. Her campaigning 'sisters' voiced criticism, but Penny's career was on the up, and she realised that she liked the attention, she liked fame, and, only a little guilty, she realised she liked flaunting her good looks and sexy curves.

She took the other interviewee chair and glanced around the studio. Just like any other, with a light wood console with the equipment recessed into it, soft pale grey carpets, and sound deadening panels covering most of the walls. A double glazed window showed the adjacent control room where a few staff were in the middle of adding milk and sugar to a tray of paper cups of tea and coffee that had just been balanced on a desk.

The presenter smiled at her. They exchanged the usual pleasantries before he held up his hand to stop the conversation, made his microphone live and, after back crediting the last piece of music, announced that he had the two actors in the studio and would be talking to them about "Faustus!".

Predictably he started the interviews by playing 'Devil May Care' and then chatted to Brian about the show, the tour and the production's success. Penny's mind wandered.

"I bet he asks about playing the most beautiful woman in the world." she thought.

"So, if I can turn to you Penny, and ask you how you feel about playing the 'face that launched a thousand ships'." the presenter said. She had guessed the wrong one of two possible opening gambits, but the general direction of the interview would be the same.

She went into a series of overworked responses to the questioning, and eventually, after they'd played her number (she was pleased about that), and told the listeners that "Faustus!" was at The Imperial from tonight and for the next four weeks, she and Brian were free to go.

"See you at the tech run." he said to her as they left the radio station.

He gave her a little pat on the shoulder as they parted in the doorway. She looked after him as he strode away down the street, wondering how she would react if he really tried it on. Their parts in the show threw them intimately together. Would she welcome that sort of relationship off stage? She shrugged, turned the other way and made off into the drizzle, pulling the hood of her coat up over her shoulder length blonde hair.

Charlie Parnell left the details of plotting and crew allocation to the visiting stage management team. Monday had found him in the deepest under-stage area of 'The Imperial'. He was with one of the venue maintenance engineers in the theatre's somewhat ageing boiler-house. They were confronting a potentially major logistical problem: how to replace a huge section of the heating system's pipework without actually shutting the theatre.

Where they stood could hardly be called a room, more an arched tunnel like a London Underground station platform. It stretched from the rear of the building, on a line with the back wall of the stage, right through to a point just beyond the front doors under the pavement in South Parade.

A complex of large diameter pipes was bracketed to the sides and the roof of the space. At various points these pipes turned through right angles and joined to one of the three huge boilers that sat spaced along the tunnel. Valves and stop taps proliferated. Gauges at the front of each boiler vibrated slightly and their needles quivered with the rumbling of the burners. Circulation pumps aided the effects of convection to push the hot water round the building to the numerous radiators, and to the double bank of these in the maw of the plenum intake up above the upper floors of the foyer block where huge fans sucked the outside air through filters, over the radiators, and through wide metal ducts to ventilator inlets in the auditorium. More grilles extracted air from the theatre as it was sucked back out to the plenum system. Thermostats controlled motorised flaps so that extracted air was either re-circulated, or ejected back into the street. These thermostats detected the temperature of the air returning from the auditorium, so that when the theatre became warmer, due to the presence of the audience, cooler outside air came in, keeping the audience comfortable. Re-circulating the extracted air, when the thermostats detected a drop in temperature meant great savings in the costs of heating the huge space.

The auditorium was always kept at quite a warm temperature, partly to ensure the audience's comfort, but also because drinks and ice-cream sales, which represented a regular income for the venue, rose when an audience was warm.

It was the pipework feeding the radiator systems that Charlie was now concerned with. In its old age serious corrosion was taking hold and most were gradually furring up. Many of the pipes were cast iron, and rusting from the insides outwards. Small leaks and little rusty, calcined, weepings from joints were commonplace. Now they needed to work out a rolling replacement program that would enable them to keep the water flowing while engineers replaced section after section of pipe.

It could be done by shutting off each boiler in turn and diverting the flow of the other two temporarily.

The planning took nearly all of Monday. It was vital that the arrangements were sorted out. The plumbers had been booked and the new pipework was already delivered, lying in a gleaming pile along the length of the boiler house. So it was a hot dry dusty Monday in the boiler-house, unwelcome despite the chill wet weather outside. Charlie was glad to reach the foyer café for a cup of tea. He arrived just about the same time as the tech run finished, and met up with many of the resident crew.

"Run through go all right?" he asked Ben.

"There's a really fast scene change in Act 2," Ben told him, "but we've sorted it out now."

"So they're happy?"

"...eh?"
"I asked if they were happy."

"Yes, it's fine, no problems." said Ben, but he wasn't really listening. He was watching Megan buying a sandwich from the café counter.

"Oi. Pay attention when I'm talking to you."

"Sorry. Just thinking."

"Yes, and I know what you were thinking." Charlie laughed.

A phone rang behind the counter and moments later the cashier shouted across to Charlie,

"It's for you!"

"It would be!"

It was the stage door, to tell him that the fire brigade had arrived for one of their regular routine inspections.

"I hope you've left everything nice and tidy for them." Charlie said to Ben as he gulped down some of his tea on his way to the door.

"Yes, we've even swept up." Ben told him. But Charlie was gone.

His place was taken, almost immediately, by Megan, steered there by Jane, who, in her self appointed role as matchmaker, had been quick to see that Ben was suddenly on his own.

The three of them had hardly said hello when Jane, looking across the room, spotted John Mason. He was heading towards the licensed part of the counter. Without a word Jane was out of her seat and had crossed the room to steer John gently by the elbow towards the café counter, where she bought him a coffee. Her departure left Ben and Megan alone. Several members of the crew in the café at the time noticed, and grinned.

By half past six that Monday evening no-one at 'The Imperial' had much time for socialising. With the opening night of "Faustus!" just an hour away the foyer areas were starting to fill with the early arrivers among the audience. Bar shutters were pushed up. Programme sales counters and souvenir and sweet kiosks opened. In the auditorium last minute checks were made, and on stage the crew's final tests were accompanied by the sounds of members of the cast, clustered around the musical director near the pit rail, doing vocal 'warm-ups'.

There would be no school parties at the opening night. The house comprised a familiar mixture of regular theatre-goers, and show virgins. The regulars were generally less likely to disrupt the smooth running of the process of seating the house ready for the start of the show. Experienced in the building's layout, and the conventional practices of box-offices, bars and programme sales they could be dealt with swiftly, though politely, and would not generally obstruct passage-ways or counters by getting lost.

First timers were another matter, and "Faustus!" was attracting a considerable proportion of its audience from the normally non-theatre-going sections of the public. They were attracted by the hype surrounding the show, and by the recent success of musical numbers from the score. Individuals, couples and families, who would not usually visit a theatre, or in some cases had never done so, now clustered into the front of house spaces.

Sometimes lost and bemused they would pass a programme

sales point, and then double back against the flow having changed their minds and decided to buy. They failed to realise that further opportunities for programmes and souvenirs would present themselves at almost every doorway.

Confused by theatre layouts, some would stray to the wrong entrances, either on the wrong floor, or on the wrong side of the house, for their seat. This resulted in the ushering staff having to redirect them 'up a floor', 'down a floor' or 'round the other side'.

The staff were familiar with this situation, and fielded the errors, and the repeated requests for information, usually 'where are the loos?' with efficient courtesy. They might laugh about some of the more glaring mistakes among themselves once the show was under way, but most incidents were so run of the mill that they passed without comment.

By about ten to seven the stage was cleared, the front of house tabs and the ad-rag flown in. A preset lighting state warmed the red velvet drapes that hid the first scene and the house-lights, and the chandelier twinkled brightly over the auditorium.

Megan phoned the front of house manager and told him 'Your house', a formal courtesy call that handed the auditorium into his control.

Word was passed to the staff next to the various entrance doors and the waiting audience was allowed into its seats.

Megan pressed the spring loaded switch on the stage manager's desk as the clock showed five to seven, bent slightly towards the mic and announced:

"Ladies and gentlemen this is your half hour call. Half an hour please. Thank you."

In the dressing rooms this routine announcement, broadcast from a loudspeaker in every room, and in places along corridors, barely registered on the cast. Their pre-show preparations were under way. Costumes were donned, make-up applied, radio mic packs fitted into the secret pockets sewn into the garments and tiny discreet mics stuck into the edges of hairlines.

She turned to a new page in the show's log and noted the date and that this was performance number two hundred and forty-nine. She wrote in 'time up' on the page ready. "Faustus!" was about to start its run at The Imperial.

Chapter 7

"A triumphant opening night at the city's Imperial theatre for "Faustus!" saw the audience on its feet for a performance that was a theatrical tour-de-force..."

John Mason stopped reading out the rave review that had appeared in the local evening paper and glanced at Megan,

"Blah blah blah.." he finished.

"Well I think it's good," she said, taking the paper from his hand. "it encourages the cast".

And she grabbed a pair of scissors and cut the review from the page and slipped it into the next empty plastic sleeve in the ring binder full of similar reviews lying on the stage management dressing room work surface.

In the staff room of the Thomas Lincoln School Miss Robinson was reading the same review to John Scarings. He and Patsy flinched slightly before her vehemence. Miss Robinson had reached a point further down the article.

"....in the second act, where stunning effects are married with some of the raunchiest dance routines ever seen in this city. The daring costumes and throbbing rock music may owe little to Christopher Marlowe, but are crowd pleasing in the extreme."

She pursed her lips and looked at the other two teachers. It was a look that said 'I told you so' with no need for the sentiment to be voiced.

"Well it seems a very good review." said John weakly.

"It seems as though you've booked a party of teenage school children into a totally unsuitable display of gratuitous flesh.

And it says it owes nothing to Marlowe"

"Perhaps the paper is exaggerating to encourage people to book." Patsy ventured.

"It's fully booked, as well you know. I trust that you two will be able to deal with the parents' complaints when they inevitably arrive." snapped Miss Robinson. "I warned you of this, but you wouldn't listen. I was against this from the start." And she stormed out of the room.

John picked up the paper.

"Brian Marsden's Faustus' sexual attraction for Helen, played by glamour model and rising star Penny Abbott is both understandable and believable and gives the audience the couple's suggestive, and now famously successful, hit duet 'The Devil in Me'..."

He shrugged.

"Oh well. I expect Year 10 will enjoy it."

"There are some members of Year 10 who'll love something raunchy." muttered Patsy. In her mind she saw a mental image of the more overtly leering boys and tarty girls in the classes.

"....and great ensemble work from the talented chorus."

read Sandy James, to the inmates of dressing room twelve, which was home to about a third of the male chorus.

"Hooray! An actual mention". said one, rather bitchily

Tuesday. Megan wrote the date, and performance two hundred and fifty. The company felt a slight frisson at passing another landmark, though Tuesday was never an exciting day, as it missed the thrill of an opening night and the audience was never quite up to the standard of the end of the week houses.

Megan had a couple of other things on her mind for that performance.

In the first case she'd decided that she did rather like Ben, and had made a bit of an effort with her appearance, sorting out her smartest black stage clothes, and paying some attention to doing her hair prior to tonight's show. Jane had noticed, and pulled her leg gently about it. The effort was almost immediately wasted as putting the talk-back headset on her head flattened her hair out again.

Her other slight distraction revolved around setting up the arrangements for playing chess. She'd found a willing challenger in one of the follow-spot operators, but the logistics of his having a chess set beside him and knowing when, and when not, to take his eyes off the stage and study his board were having to be worked out. Megan, of course, knew the show backwards and had her hands free anyway except for occasional switch pressing. They'd try a quick game tonight, and she'd give him longer standbys than would otherwise be the case.

In the event chess took a back seat that night.

After she'd called the half Megan went back to the stage management dressing room, and discovered, to her annoyance, a text on her phone, from Tom, announcing that the latest bill was for the electricity in the flat, and that he had no way of paying it.

Once the show was running there were a succession of tiny glitches.

Theatre people sometimes refer to these as 'second night

blues', but 'Faustus!' had been running for so long that this hardly counted as an excuse. True the audience were unaware of any   problems. However the setbacks wounded her pride in her work, though none of the difficulties were of her making.

Act one started with a problem with a radio mic that saw Megan leaving the prompt corner and having to delve down the back of the costume of one of the singing chorus members to switch on a transmitter pack that had mysteriously got turned off.

She had no sooner returned to the prompt desk and made a note of the incident in the log, than one of the on-stage group's combo amplifiers blew a fuse. This was not during a musical number that involved them, fortunately, and some frantic screwdriver work by Ben, and Charlie, who arrived with remarkable prescience, on hands and knees concealed from the audience by the handrail on the group's raised dais, put all back into working order in time.

Some strange, and totally inexplicable set of circumstances moved one of the CCTV cameras, so that her view of some parts of the stage from the prompt desk was unavailable, and correction of that took much of the interval. They agreed to blame a failure to tighten a locking bolt for the movement, but no-one could really explain how this had happened with such a routine piece of rigging.

Megan was pleased when Act two got smoothly under way, and was beginning to relax again when the real crisis of the evening occurred. In the scene change that The Imperial's crew had identified as being fast it was necessary for the crew to drop the sprung locking pivot pin on the bottom of the various trucks into the drillings in the touring show's false stage floor. They were unable to do this on the downstage prompt truck. The show ploughed on, and Megan, cans still on her head, was on her knees in the wings, her head right on the floor, trying to look underneath the truck to see what the problem was. With mere seconds to go before the truck was due to swivel on this pivot the struggling crew got the pin to drop into place.

As she was about to get up she felt a pair of hands on her bottom.

"Ah! My favourite girl. You don't have to bow down to me." whispered the joking voice of Frank Durban in her ear.

There was, actually, no need to whisper. "Faustus!" ran at a sound level that made it unlikely that any audience could hear a conversation in the wings, but most cast and crew adopted lowered tones out of habit.

She looked up. Frank's smiling face was completely out of keeping with the Devil make-up and costume he was wearing.

"Truck cue 14, LX cue 178, Go!" she said down her headset mic automatically. "LX 179, Go!" she added a moment later.

"Get your hands off my bum" she told Frank mock scoldingly.

"A shame, such a pretty bum."

"LX 180, FX 23, Go!"

There was a flash and a cloud of smoke in response. The lighting changed startlingly to a vivid red and moving heads swept their beams across to point at the downstage edge of the stage near them. Simultaneously, abandoning the conversation, Frank leapt out from the wings onto his mark to be pinned by the intense light arriving through the smoke at that point.

"..and I hope that scorches your arse!" Megan said as Frank went on stage.

The music for the next number, a continuation of the last, started with a vibrant crash and the show went on.
Megan went back to her desk.

"Friend of yours?" Ben, who'd been witness to the little exchange, quizzed.

"Did you say friend, or fiend?" Megan laughed. "Don't worry..he's not my type. I like a little less brimstone. Standby LX 181"

After the show they all clustered round to look at the pin on the offending truck. They could find nothing wrong with it, but they agreed to run that scene change again tomorrow before the show. It had been a momentarily worrying, but rare, deviation from the regular smooth routine of a long running show.

Wednesday's promised examination of the truck offered no more explanation. Repeated raising and lowering of the spigot pin seemed to work perfectly. Eventually Ben, who with Charlie had been trying for some time to repeat last nights problem, squirted some silicone lubricant down the shaft of the pin and got up off his knees. He brushed his hand back and forth on his trousers, which almost miraculously, it seemed to Megan, returned to their usual smart and presentable condition.

"I don't think that there's much else we can do with it." he said.

"Come on then," she invited him, "I'll buy you a drink...Oh and you too of course, Charlie."

"You two go," Charlie replied, "I've got a mountain of

paperwork to do, and they're starting on the heating pipes immediately, so we've got to schedule the boiler changeovers."

"We've got a matinee on Friday. It's not going to be cold is it? I mean you've seen the girls' Act two costumes haven't you?"

"Oh they're costumes are they? Looked to me as though wardrobe had run out of budget." Charlie joked. "Don't worry normal service will be resumed as soon as possible. Well actually you'll never know the difference up here. Now go on, push off the pair of you before the pubs start filling up with workers leaving off."

They went to the pub on the corner at the bottom end of Wellington Street, coming out of the stage door and turning down the hill past the now closed roller shutters of the loading door. Just for the moment the rain that had seemed as if it would never end had eased to a clammy autumn drizzle and, just as Charlie had predicted, the first office workers were squelching homeward through the puddles under street-lights that were beginning to fire up in the gloomy conditions.

They found a pub that was already noisy and nearly full. Several members of the crew were there, but Megan and Ben worked their way to an empty space in a corner where they drank a hasty lager each before it was time to get ready for the evening show.

They talked little, though Megan told a couple of funny stories from incidents earlier in the tour, and Ben responded in kind with backstage tales from The Imperial. They were both at a bit of a loss how to go on with this conversation when Ben eventually asked

"Is there anything going on between you and that bloke playing the devil?"

"What Frank?" Megan laughed. "Good grief no. He's a bit touchy feely, if you know what I mean, but he knows he stands no chance."

Suddenly she started to tell Ben all about Tom, and the argument, and how she'd stormed out without even packing properly, and how she'd kept expecting him to call and apologise. About the gas bill, and now the text about the electric bill. And how she felt she'd been used as a meal ticket, stupidly paying more than her share of the household expenses, and how she really didn't know what to do. How she hoped he would move out and save her further bother, but if he did could she really afford to keep a London flat and live in digs too.

But it wasn't in her nature to be maudlin, and she noticed the noise of the bar around them getting louder.

"Come on," she said, "time to go and set up. Another house full of punters wanting to be entertained!"

They got up.

"Race you back to the stage door!" she laughed, and they ran up the street like silly children.

It seemed to Ben that he hadn't done anything like that for years. The pair crashed through the stage door into the little lobby. Stan was already behind the glass with the usual evening door keeper, Oliver.

"Bloody hell! The youth of today." Oliver, a loud middle aged northerner, protested.

"Sorry", Megan had reached the entrance just ahead of Ben.

They were saved from more embarrassment by several more cast members arriving.

"Don't tell me our Ben's got himself a girlfriend." Stan said to Oliver after the group had disappeared towards the dressing rooms.

Chapter 8

On Thursday Paula Morley's Aunt mentioned the dust again to her fellow cleaners.

"Well luv, you've got to expect dust with all these people coming in and out."

"Oh I know that, but this is funny stuff." she grumbled.

"Anyway," said another, "I'd rather have dust than the ice cream tubs. Nasty sticky things"

"Chewing gum's the worst."

"Too right." chorused the assembled women.

Paula's Aunt shrugged, and went off into the stalls bar to wipe the glass of the counter display cabinets. She would take the opportunity to pocket a couple of chocolate bars to give to her niece. She worried a bit about Paula. Paula was so skinny. She could do with a good feeding up the woman decided. If her sister fed the girl properly she'd have some proper fat on her, instead of looking like a stick. Theirs wasn't a family of slim catwalk models. Theirs was a family of big cuddly women, and the husbands appreciated it. Why the girl was such a waif was a mystery.

In the cellars two plumbers were supposed to be removing one section of the pipework in the boiler house.

They were sitting on their toolboxes drinking coffee, on the excuse that they had to wait for the, now shut down, boiler three to cool. This was completely untrue, as Charlie had shut the boiler down himself at the end of the Wednesday night performance, but at this early hour even Charlie had not yet arrived. The plumbers had been let in by Stan, who was at the end of his shift. They were now the only occupants of the building apart from the cleaners and a daytime door-keeper. By the time Charlie did come in to work the two idlers had made a rather half hearted start on stripping the lagging from the pipe.

He chatted with them for a while and tried to impress on them the need to get to suitable points in the work in time for each performance. He was not naive enough to think that his words would have any effect. He'd spent some time getting prices for this work over the past months, and had been forced, by the theatre management, into taking the cheapest quote. He'd known this would be a mistake. As he left the boiler-house he decided he had been right. Anyway it was no good worrying about it, he would just have to keep an eye on them. They had, at least, been able to start work almost at once.

Behind him the plumbers returned to stripping lagging from the elderly pipework. It was a dirty job. Strictly they should have been wearing considerable amounts of protective clothing, but they were unobserved, and contented themselves with tying their handkerchiefs around their mouths to keep the worst of the dust out at bay. It made them look like outlaws in old western films. The irony of their being cowboys was lost on them.

They would spend most of the day in the hot gloom of the boiler-room. When they undid the first section of pipe a dirty puddle of rusty water formed on the floor. When they dragged the section out from it's place piles of flakes of calcined fur from the insides cascaded to the concrete and if you looked into the tube you could see that the solid fur had reduced the effective bore by more than half.

By the end of the working day they were in the process of cutting the new replacement pipes to match the section they'd removed.

Leaving a gaping hole in the theatre's heating system, they ascended to the stage door and went home.

Dan watched his wife putting a few things into an overnight bag. He knew that she was worried and upset about her father's state. He didn't know what to say to her. Always a bit clumsy and awkward with emotions he held back from offering a comment in case he got it wrong.

Alison turned from her packing.

"Well, that will do for a couple of days. I'll have to go. If I don't get the next bus I'll miss the train."

Dan had offered to drive her to the station in the van of course, but the practicalities of of fitting Simon in too were too great. Anyway the rush hour traffic was starting to block the streets, and the bus would make better time, using bus lanes, than he could with a small lorry. The family car was long gone, a part trade in against the van.

"Now you're sure you'll be all right." she fussed. "There's something for tonight's tea in the fridge, and I've done a stew for you for tomorrow night, all you need to do is heat it up. I suppose you'll get something on the road during the day tomorrow ..."

He knew that all this was really just a cover for her upset at what awaited in Scotland.

"We'll be fine. Say goodbye to your mum, Simon."

"Bye mum." said Simon, unaffected by the parting, and unaware of the cause.

"Give mummy a hug" said Alison, and got a reluctant quick squeeze from her son before he wriggled off to carry on playing.

Dan hugged his wife.

"I hope it goes well." he said weakly.

"So do I. Goodbye. And take care of Simon. Don't let him stay up too late." she turned again at the door, "Oh, and make sure he cleans his teeth properly, he just sucks his toothbrush if you don't help him."

"I will."

"Bye Simon, bye darling."

The door slammed shut and Alison made towards the bus stop.

Ignoring the instruction about 'something for tea in the fridge' Dan said to his son,

"How about McDonalds for tea?"

"Wow! Yeah Dad!"

So they went.

John Scarings stuffed papers into his briefcase in the staff room of the Thomas Lincoln School. He'd done his best. He'd tried to make sure that all the pupils who were going to the show tomorrow knew roughly what time they would be coming back, and had arranged for their parents to meet them if they lived too far away. Letters had been sent home, but most would be screwed up in the bottom of bags or pockets.

"Looking forward to it Patsy?" he asked.

"It sounds very risqué." she said.

If truth be told she was uncertain about the whole expedition now. When it had first been booked it was an attractive idea, an escape from her self imposed social isolation, an opportunity to see a show. And if that had to involve marshalling an army of truculent school children, well so be it. She would not be alone. John was a good teacher, and Nick Arthur had a boisterous and outgoing enough personality to control almost any gathering of pupils.

It was the reviews that were concerning her now. Not just those in the local press, but the ones that had steadily found their way into the nationals ever since the tour had started. She had read more and more about the show since the trip had been organised.

'Raunchy', 'sexy'. 'semi-naked' all seemed to feature as prominent words in these reviews. She knew, in her deepest mind, that these words were used by reporters and reviewers to inject zest into their pieces for the readership. She knew too that this sort of vocabulary was employed to help to swell audiences.

However these were also the sort of words that embarrassed her. She was naturally shy and withdrawn. In the privacy of her own bathroom she tucked her dressing gown tightly around herself. She blushed at the crude conversations of the pupils. They knew this and would frequently and deliberately bring up topics that she wished to avoid. She went to some lengths in the modern world to avoid the prevalent exposure of flesh, in magazines, on screen, in newspapers... and now it seemed on stage. However she had not failed to see several of Penny's glamour pictures turning up in print and wondered at how any woman could pose like that. Aside from so nearly showing Penny's most intimate parts these pictures made Patsy flush with embarrassment at how clearly the positions adopted were supposed to show a desire for sex.

"I don't know if it's going to turn out to be suitable for the pupils." she qualified.

"They'll love it. Sex and rock and roll. Two out of the usual three should hold their interest." He saw her slightly horrified expression. "Sorry, that was supposed to be a joke."

"Can I ask you something?"

"Of course"

"Can I come with you on your bus and let Tigger and Miss Robinson go on the other one?"

"I don't see why not" he agreed, "are you trying to avoid our revered Miss Robinson?"

"She just orders me about so. I don't want to go to a show all upset right from the start.... even if it does sound a bit as though I may find it too, well 'saucy' perhaps."

"Silly girl." and he surprised her by reaching out and squeezing her hand, just as Tigger came in. She felt herself start to blush, and a stray thought that perhaps John would secretly like her to display herself with scraps of material barely covering her and her hips thrust forward inviting him to take her flashed into her mind.

For once Nick Arthur said nothing, though his eyebrows raised slightly, and the pair had no doubt that he'd noticed. Patsy snatched her hand away, ashamed of her split second fantasy.

"Everything in order for the herding exercise tomorrow?" asked Tigger.

"Herding?"

"Have you ever tried to control a bus load of kids, young lady? It's like herding, but herding cats."

"Mr Scarings and I will be fine on our bus." she quickly sought a way to establish the distribution of personnel in the way she'd hoped for.

"Oh no! I'll ride herd on all the kids you like, even 10D if I must, but spare me the wicked witch."

"We thought..." Patsy started, dismayed, but Tigger burst out laughing.

"It's all right, I can deal with wicked witches. You young people want to be together."

Patsy blushed properly now.

She thought about what Nick Arthur had said all the way home to her flat, Did he really think....

Dan and Simon sat in the colourful plastic child world, and Dan watched his son eagerly tucking in to McSomething-or-others and fries. He personally would have preferred proper chips, but knew that Simon liked this rare treat. Absently he pulled another 'fry' out of the little cardboard container. It wouldn't have been cold if it had been a proper chip from the local 'chippy' he thought.

In the privacy of her bedroom Gemma Barents had no qualms about fantasising over John Scarings. Her schoolbooks were scattered around her, but she lay back on her bed ignoring them as her hand rested on the front of her skirt and rubbed gently.. In her mind a smiling Mr Scarings was above her, patient, attentive and loving in all the senses of the word.

Chapter 9

"Ladies and gentlemen, this is your half hour call. Half an hour please."

Up and down the passageways and staircases of The Imperial's ageing backstage, in every dressing room, and in the green room Megan's recital of the worn old mantra could be heard, with a slight echo in those places where the listener might catch the output of two loudspeakers.

The Thursday night performance drew close. In the orchestra pit the percussionist tutted and blew some dust off the covers of his timpani. It seemed to him that The Imperial was a particularly dirty venue. No-one else in the pit orchestra seemed to be having the same trouble with muck. As usual they had each established a sort of personal camp around their particular seat, mic stand and music stand. Paperback books and Kindles were commonplace. There was a pack of cards in use among the brass section, and universal throughout the length of the pit were drinks bottles and sandwiches. No one else had got dust in their sandwiches. He looked about, expecting to find an air inlet vent blowing onto his space that he could block up. There was none.

On stage the electric part of the orchestra, on their platform built into the set, plugged in guitars and electric basses and turned on keyboards and combo amps. A few experimental twangs proved that "Faustus!"'s on-stage band was readying itself for the next performance.

Megan wrote 'performance 252' on the page for tonight's show.

Front of house the audience poured into the auditorium, found their seats, bought and read their programmes, sucked sweets, and gazed around The Imperial's decorative auditorium and at the mass of lighting and sound equipment hanging in it.

Some of them read the cast list in the programme. Few turned to the pages that showed the long lists of technical staff both touring with the show, and working for The Imperial.

Eventually the front of house tannoys called the audience to 'take your seats now please', and Megan's call for 'act one beginners' echoed around the back stage of the building. The advertising rag flew out into the roof void to reveal the theatre's expanse of rich, red, velvet drapes.

The cast, orchestra and crew waited to start. The conductor looked toward the CCTV camera, knowing Megan was watching him on the monitor. He winked at her and grinned. It was unorthodox, but it saved him putting headphones on to tell her all was ready in the pit. House-lights faded, and the overture began.

An overture combines several, sometimes all, the numbers from the show, in a medley designed to familiarise the audience with the tunes before they hear them in the show itself. With "Faustus!" many of those numbers were already very familiar to the audience, from repeated airplay on radio and television, and from the chart success of some of them.

As a result The Imperial's audience tapped its feet and even clapped along with the hit numbers where they appeared in the overture. So the curtain rose nightly to a house filled with customers with a warm and appreciative attitude to the show from the outset.

Thursday night was just the same.

A roar of applause greeted the tabs flying out to herald the opening scene. The set, configured to be a medieval street scene, with a cut-away frontage of Dr Faustus' study below the on-stage group's raised podium. The opening number, 'Always Working', involved almost the entire company, chorus and dancers in medieval costumes in an up-tempo introduction to the title character's obsessive studying.

Megan rattled through the first few minutes, knowing that a moderately lengthy piece of text followed this opening number, and determined that she'd get a couple of moves of her chess game with the lime operator played before the next series of cues.

'Always Working' finished to applause, and a lighting change shifted attention from from the massed chorus to Brian Marsden. He had been framed in a followspot's beam for the last few bars of the song, but now walked downstage from beneath the group. The lime faded out and was replaced by several moving heads which swung round to pin him in an upturned pyramid of visible beams. Head twenty-three joined the others a split second late. Alistair cursed under his breath. He would have to have another look at that mover if it got any worse. When the lime faded out its operator was free to say "d5" in response to Megan's opening move.

The next short scene would satisfy Miss Robinson's conservative views on adapting the classics when she saw it. In principle it was the Marlowe play's opening prologue, in which the chorus sets the background, and tells the audience what is about to happen. In "Faustus!" the 'chorus' character was positioned on the upstage raised platform, just next to the band. He perched on the handrail and addressed the audience in a casual but commanding way that had led some critics to draw comparisons with the 'lead player' in 'Pippin'.

Brian had few lines in this section, though he was the centre of attention. By the time he was coming to his first number Megan was looking at the permutations offered by black's 'Queen to f6' which had followed the first couple of moves.

Brian's loyal fans applauded his number 'What use is science', but were thrilled by the segue into the popular following number 'All humans sin'.

Charlie came out onto the little balcony near the proscenium and watched a few minutes of the show from there. He much preferred musicals to straight plays. During the run of the show here, he promised himself, he would actually see the whole thing all the way through uninterrupted. Just now the pressures   of running the building were occupying both his time and his thoughts. The heating and plumbing featured much in his pondering. Yes, the house was warm enough, he thought, almost instinctively checking as he stood there. But there were a few minor faults that had cropped up in the past week that needed chasing up, and management was pressuring for a report on a refurbishment of the advertising cabinets and hoardings front of house.

As the show carried on there was another lighting cue involving the moving heads close beside his eyrie. Despite the sound level of the show, it was the start of a sequence of summonsings that punctuate Dr Faustus and a chorus number entitled 'Black and White' in which good and bad angels exchange views on Faustus' interest in magic, he could hear a squeak as one of the moving heads re-positioned itself.

When he later mentioned the noise to Ben, as they stood at the bar of the pub round the corner after the show, Ben said,

"Nodding buckets. The damn things make all sorts of noises."

"That's why shows are so loud these days." Tim chipped in.

"Are you getting old? Starting to tell the youngsters to turn it down?"

"Well if they cut it down a bit I wouldn't have to fly so much

PA for them." Tim joked.

"Anything for a quiet life. We all know you spend all your time sleeping on that fly floor."

Ben had spent much of the performance, as he now did for each performance, partly due to his duties on stage, and partly to watch Megan, in the prompt side wing. He was mildly amused by the routine she adopted, calling cues at speed in the show's fraught moments, and turning back to the chess game in each lull. He thought about her quite a lot now. Her revelation of the failure of her long term relationship had made him consider her in a very different way. He enjoyed her company, and their occasional drink in the pub. He was also honest enough with himself to admit that she had become a fantasy at night.

They arrived at the sequence for the seven deadly sins. This had been written as a small oratorio. In earlier times it would have been released as a 'concept album', now it had become a popular item on playlists with DJs picking and choosing preferred passages from pride, greed, lust, envy, gluttony, anger and sloth.

The show's cast, roughly divided into seven sections for this, each group having both singers and dancers. It was one moment in the show where the much advertised raunchiness of the costumes, and indeed, in the case of lust, the dance routines, was unleashed on the waiting audiences.

Scintillating flowing costumes of silk and lamé filled the stage for the slow parading choreography of pride, making way seamlessly for the grasping arm movements of the dancers in greed, and then the traditional shades of green in the envy section.

The audience clapped along to the now hugely familiar gluttony section and was enthralled by the slow balletic sloth movement.

The producers had adjusted the order of the 'sins' during the tour, and the anger and lust numbers were now the final parts of the section.

Obedient to Megan's lighting cues the lighting rig colour changed to reds with sharp moving beams slashing through the smoke. The onstage rock band took the musical lead and the dancers, in scanty military armour performed their counter-marching routines to the rousing lyric. There was thunderous applause. But it was lust that the audience was waiting for.

The rig cross faded to shades of purple, with slowly rotating beams of light picking out the now almost naked dancers in a routine that had aroused some protests at its pelvis thrusting simulation of copulation. The audience knew this musical number probably better than any other in the show. There had not been quite so much public reaction to a stage musical number since 'Hair' had opened in the permissive sixties. The music for this part of "Faustus!" had made its way onto TV and radio broadcasts. Pirate videos of the dance routine had escaped onto the internet. One or two brave late night broadcasters had shown carefully selected clips from the live show DVD by arrangement.

At all points in the show the audience was swept along by the pulsating rhythms and visual effects. The cast, and the orchestra and band, sweated through the numbers. Throughout Megan called sequences of cues, though many were programmed to follow each other, 'follow-ons' as they were known, in seamless pre-plotted succession. As the final crashing chords of one piece shook the venerable old Imperial the sections of the set trucked aside to reveal a central flight of treads, suddenly and brilliantly lit in white light, with Penny, as Helen of Troy, standing at the top.

Brian, who'd been no more than a bystander to the previous sequence to this, launched straight into the yearning melody of 'Make Me Immortal' so the audience was led from one hit number to another, from one musical style to another, from one sentiment to another with no time to draw breath.

And Megan made another chess move over the headset system.

Ben looked across at Helen of Troy. As the sequence started she stood on the staircase, clad in a tight, thin, flesh coloured body suit with a sheer diaphanous robe over it. The robe hid none of her body, and a necklace and bracelets concealed the places where the body stocking ended and Penny's skin began. A pair of the moving head lights were focussed with rippling gobos in their gates exaggerated the fluttering of her robe as it blew out in an artificial breeze. The impression that the actress was naked, but for carefully placed scraps, was total. It was set-piece moments like these that were helping to produce the salacious headlines to reviews that the show was earning.

Penny was, thought Ben, almost too perfect a model figure. He could see why the media and the photographers had become so enamoured of her, and having exchanged a few words with her backstage during the past week he was impressed by her lack of ego. Most stars, in his experience, and especially those on a meteoric rise to public acclaim, developed a self absorbed attitude. Perhaps, he though, that was what pushed them onward towards stardom in the first place. Either way he deduced that Penny was a much more pleasant and down to earth actress than her present billing would have suggested.

He became aware that several other members of the Imperial's crew were in the gloom, clearly absorbed in the view.

Looking back towards the prompt desk he saw that Megan was watching him, while she waited for a chess move to come back down the headphones from her opponent. He turned away from the stage, guilty, like a schoolboy caught ogling a glossy porn magazine.

Brian was starting the last verse and chorus of 'Make me immortal'.

"Having a good look?" asked Megan.

She had seen so many crew members lurk in the wings for parts of this show, particularly this part of this show, over the past few months that it provided some amusement to her. She and Jane regularly had a casual competition to guess which crew members would hang around in the wings the most. She hadn't had Ben on her voyeur list.

"No, no, er I was just...."

"You were 'just'!"

"She's too skinny for me. I like girls more cuddly..."

"Good God! Now you're saying I'm fat!"

"No. No. I meant...it was supposed to be..."

She laughed at his confusion.

This was, they both realised a tacit admission that he liked her and she knew it. Ben was saved by the end of the number, and a succession of cues that kept Megan busy for the next few moments.

It was some hilarity that Megan told Jane about this exchange later as they packed up for the night in the stage management dressing room.

"I told you he fancied you." insisted Jane. "He would think I'm too skinny too."

"I was thinking about going on a diet. I might as well save myself the misery if he likes me fat."

Ben knocked on the open door of the dressing room. If he had heard he showed no sign.

"Anyone coming for a drink?" he asked.

"I'm going home," said Jane quickly, "I'll leave you two together." and she grabbed her coat and bag and was gone, slamming the door behind her

Megan laughed again. Perhaps it was the easy sense of humour that made her so appealing to him he thought.

"Oh come here." she said. And she reached out and kissed him.

When they left she remembered she'd left her hairbrush on the prompt desk. They paused at the stage as they made their way to the stage door. Ben held the door to the prompt side passageway open as Megan went in to fetch her brush. As she turned to leave she looked up at the single light bulb glowing above the desk, and reached out to the switch on the steel conduit that ran down from it and flicked it off. Framed in the doorway lit from the passageway behind him Ben said,

"No, leave that one on."

Megan clicked the switch again. The bulb flashed momentarily, and there was a faint ping as the filament failed.

"I think the lamp's gone." she said.

"Damn. And electrics will have gone home by now."

"They can do it in the morning."

"I don't like to leave it," said Ben, "but I expect the sparks have locked up too, so I can't get at the spares."

At the stage door he said to Stan behind the glass of the stage door keeper's hutch,

"Mind how you go tonight. The ghost light has failed."

"Can't you fix it?"

"No spares. But you've got a torch haven't you?"

"Don't worry. I won't fall in the orchestra pit. But I don't like it. It's bad luck."

"I know, but we'll have to risk it." Ben seemed reluctant, "Night Stan."

As they walked away Megan asked, "What did you mean 'bad luck'?"

Ben seemed surprised.

"You don't know about ghost lights?"

She shook her head, "Tell me." she said, taking hold of his arm with both hands,

"Well most old theatres have ghost lights. Normally they're in the middle of the stage, ours is a bit unusual being in the prompt side wing. They're probably really for exactly what Stan said, to stop people falling into the pit during the night. But everyone says they're to look after the theatre ghost."

"Ghost? Has The Imperial got one?"

"Nearly all old theatres have one, and they like to perform at night, and they can't do that in the dark, so we leave a ghost light on so as not to upset them."

"I suppose you'll tell me next that's because they can't turn it on themselves if they want it."

"Well of course not. They can't hold things. I gather the ones at the Palace in London like to sit in the auditorium, and as they can't flip the tip-up seats down they have a couple of them fixed down during the night. On the balcony somewhere I think."

"Now I know you're making this up." said Megan, and punched him jokingly on the upper arm.

"Anyway," Ben rubbed his arm where she'd hit him, "it's bad luck not to have a ghost light on overnight."

And they walked on into the wet city streets.

In London Tom finished his shift in the bar. On the tube journey back to the flat he mused yet again about the failure of his relationship with Megan and the financial straits it had put him in. Finally he had made up his mind. Texting had not worked. A face to face approach was needed. He would get a train and ask her to come back. He would do it tomorrow.

Chapter 10

If Gemma Barrents' mother noticed the extra care that her daughter took over her preparations for school the next morning she made no comment. Gemma was very conscious of the forthcoming theatre trip, and the possibility of spending time in the company of John Scarings. So she took great pains with her preparations, particularly packing make-up and some jewellery into her school bag. She added a toothbrush and toothpaste Although it was a Friday she'd arranged that her school uniform was freshly laundered and ironed, which would probably only normally have been the case for all of it on a Monday, and picked out her best underwear.

Gemma was under no real illusions. She knew that she would be in a crowd with Mr Scarings, but was hopeful that she might manage to arrange the seating in the theatre so that she was next to the object of her crush. She imagined them seated side by side in the dark auditorium, perhaps holding hands, with the surrounding audience a sort of out of focus background in the gloom of her fantasy. She day-dreamed of him being smiling and attentive to her, just like in her bedroom imagination. She studied herself in the mirror on the back of her wardrobe door wriggled her hips, tried to see herself from the sides and straightened her skirt. She tried lifting her long hair up, then let it drop back into its usual place over her shoulders. Her indecision was cut short by her mother's instruction to her to 'hurry up'.

They exchanged brief morning greetings, and Gemma made sure that her mother had remembered about the theatre trip. She would be back, she promised, by early evening. The school hadn't told the pupils exactly what time the show would finish, but it had announced that the buses would be back at the school about half past seven, the time the curtain would be rising on the evening performance. The school was attending the matinee.

Gemma left the house with her bag over her shoulder. Like most modern school children she neglected to take a coat with her despite the drizzling rain.

There were several other girls and boys of varying ages at the bus stop and eventually they all piled onto the bus that headed off on a circuitous journey through the suburbs towards the Thomas Lincoln School. Gemma said 'hello' to a couple of the girls, and pointedly ignored the evident admiration of three younger boys with a upward tilt of her head and a slight flick of her hair as she seated herself.

Patsy dressed in one of her traditionally sombre grey outfits before making her way to the school. Despite her concerns about the possible style of "Faustus!" and its raunchy reputation she found that she was eager for the day to pass so she could see the show. Certainly there was a down side. The pupils would be a nuisance she knew. The boys particularly worried her. Her classroom discipline was shaky at best and she felt no confidence in her ability to control them in a strange location.

She could hardly stand up in the middle of a crowded auditorium and shout at them, she thought. John would have to sort them out. She started slightly. She'd thought of him as 'John', not Mr. Scarings, in a school context. That was quite unlike her. She carefully compartmentalised her thoughts and would never risk the chance of using what she saw as the wrong appellation in conversation at work. Her thinking about John was still confused and repressed.

Reluctantly she turned in through the school gates and trudged up the main drive to the door nearest to the staircase that led to the staff room. Pupils pushed past her, some even actually brushing against her without acknowledging her existence. Glad to reach sanctuary she went in to the staff room.

"....and the buggers have said I've got to go with the old bat."
Tigger was telling the scattering of staff members in the
room.

He waved a steaming kettle at her as she came in.

"Speak of the devil, well one of them." he greeted her
unabashed, "Coffee before the misery of the white board?"

"Please."

"We used to talk about a hard day at the chalk face, you
know," he went on, stirring instant coffee powder into hot
water, "but they can't afford chalk any more, which is a pity,
because it was good ammunition if you wanted to throw
something at the little terrors. You do have it white don't
you?"

Patsy took the offered mug. It didn't seem any too clean, so
she turned it round to drink out of the other side, discovering
that it had 'I used to be uncertain, now I'm not so sure' printed
on it. Suddenly she found a seam of confidence. With Tigger
and Mr Scarings along perhaps she wouldn't need to show
any leadership or take any decisions. The show might be
enjoyable after all. Tigger's outgoing personality was
infecting her, at least until the bell rang for the start of the
school day a couple of minutes later. Her first lesson of the
day with some of Year 10 gave her an inkling of the mixed
reactions of the pupils to the day's theatre trip.

In the flat walled, pastel coloured classroom the boys were
the most disinterested, calling the show 'minging' and 'naff'
without having seen it. It would be distinctly un-cool to
express any enthusiasm, and peer pressure was rife.

Some of the girls, especially those who were in dance
schools or fancied themselves as performers were a bit more
receptive.

It was when the slightly rowdy classroom discussion of the event strayed into the area of speculation about the sexy content that Patsy found herself as an unwilling referee in an argument that seemed to reverse the type cast roles. The boys found that the prospect of seeing naked female flesh was interesting, despite their antipathy towards the educational 'Dr. Faustus' related content. Their potential voyeurism produced typical and predictable disgust and disdain from the girls in the class.

Patsy's embarrassment at the whole topic had her fighting to cut the discussion short to return the lesson to its proper course. The pupils reluctantly dropped the conversation, but Patsy had been horrified at what some of the boys had seemed to want from the show. She was acutely aware of burning heat in her face as she tried to steer the lesson along safe lines that would not bring out her timidity.

Dan was being frustrated by Simon's lack of urgency. Dan wanted to be out of the house and starting on the day of deliveries. The child was pushing the breakfast cereal around his bowl with the spoon in one hand but concentrating on wheeling his toy lorry across the table with the other. To watch the toy from a better angle he had laid his head on the table on one side, and there was an imminent risk of the bowl and its contents being tipped over.

"Hurry up, Simon. We've got to go and get in the truck."

There was no real acceleration in the boy's eating. He took one more spoonful and returned his attention to the toy.

"Simon!"

The boy lifted his head and looked up for a moment.

"We've got to go."

"-kay Dad."

"Look I'll go and sort your seat out. Finish that before I get back."

Leaving his son to finish his breakfast, or more likely not, he thought, Dan went out to his truck and strapped a booster seat on the passenger side of the cab. He took some care and made sure the seat belt would hold the child properly. Routinely he checked the vehicle's fluid levels and wiped the mirrors and windscreen. The air was full of moisture, not rain, or even drizzle, but a constant haze that he knew would be a nuisance for the wipers. Eventually satisfied, and feeling a bit guilty at having left Simon alone a bit longer than he'd intended, he went back inside.

Simon was still at the table. Dan put the half eaten bowl beside the sink, not bothering to wash up in the haste to leave and be out on the road.

Simon, clad in his anorak and clutching the toy lorry, was lifted into the cab and strapped in. Dan shut the passenger door and walked round to the driver's side. He pulled himself up into the driving seat and started the engine.

"Ready?"

"Yeah!" Simon was excited at the prospect of riding in the truck.

His father put the vehicle in gear and released the air brakes with the stubby lever beside his seat. They moved off towards the depot where they would collect the day's load.

The delay meant that they ran into the morning rush hour traffic. Dan had hoped to have been en-route early enough to avoid that. The fork lift driver at the depot commented,

"Bit late today aren't you?"

"Yeah. I've got help with me today though, so I'm sure I'll catch up." He jerked a thumb at the other side of the cab.

"Hello." the fork lifter said through the window, "Helping Dad today are you?"

"I've got a lorry." said Simon, holding up his toy.

"So's your Dad." the man laughed "We'd better get it loaded".

And because Dan was popular at the depot the load came on board in record time and they were only a little later than usual leaving the yard for the first delivery address and heading out onto the road.

Tom was having a morning of frustrations and annoyances. An uncomfortable trip from the flat to a London main line station on underground trains jammed with morning commuters had followed a hasty breakfast. Unused in either his actor or barman careers to the hell that is London's workers fighting their way into work he was irritated beyond measure by the pushing and shoving that went with the journey. His temper had been worsening ever since his last spat with Megan. The money shortage had done nothing to mellow him. Now it seemed the population was conspiring to cause him problems. He was knocked and buffeted by brief cases and umbrellas, and most annoyingly by back packs, who's owners contrived to bang their luggage into him whenever they turned, and to be completely unaware of doing so. For his part his hesitancy at twists and turns of the capital's subterranean passageways as he found his way to the main line station frustrated regular commuters for whom specific routes were second nature, and increased the number of minor collisions.

At the main line ticket office he was now horrified at the price of the return ticket he needed. His query as to whether there was a cheaper alternative was met with indifference by the woman behind the desk and the grudging information that it would have been cheaper if he had booked some time in advance. By debating the issue he managed to be the cause of further annoyance to other travellers in the queue behind him. Now he clutched his tickets and stared up at the clattering departure board as it flicked over updating the details of the next departures. Over an hour to wait.

He loitered around the barrier guarding the indicated platform of the terminus. Though the gates he could see the empty platform and the lines snaking away into the distance. He paced about, there was nowhere to sit and wait. The very few seats were occupied by glum travellers, their eyes fixed hopefully on the information boards. His travelling in recent years had been limited to an occasional tube journey to the rare audition, and going in Megan's car with her to a supermarket for a big shop on ever less frequent Sunday expeditions. His bar work was always found within walking distance of the flat and he shopped at local small shops.

He'd forgotten the frustrations of public transport. If he hadn't convinced himself that the journey to win Megan round was vital for his financial and living comfort, and perhaps, if he was honest with himself, for his occasional sexual satisfaction, for he found he still lusted after her curvy body, he would have given up the day's trip. Part of him wished he'd not spent the money. Part of him was sure it was a good investment. It was an ambivalent way to start the day.

Eventually wandering back towards the barrier he could see an approaching train, nosing its way towards the buffers. As it drew to a halt doors along its entire length burst open and a wave of passengers came straight towards him. He saw that station staff were manning the gates, to allow the arrivals out, but to prevent new passengers from getting on to the platform.

The first through the barrier were the runners, hurrying for taxis, for the underground, to work or to anticipated fun or entertainment. He dodged this vanguard easily. He pondered the perceived injustice of those who might be heading to watch shows passing by him. He, who still resented not being one of the performers they were rushing to see that evening. His mind refused to accept that he might not be as talented as those who were in work. He believed he was passed over unfairly. He had managed to convince himself over months of resting that a conspiracy existed. This, he was sure, was tied to a system of preference ingrained in the casting process. It was not, he told himself talent but jobs for the boys, or girls, that created a cast. He was certain that directors regularly cast their friends or lovers.

Occupied by these bitter reflections he failed to notice the huge dense mass of the major part of the disembarking passengers as it swept towards him, and was pushed and shoved for the second time that day. His bitterness seethed. Further annoyed by not being allowed to board the now waiting train he stamped off and bought himself a newspaper. By the time he returned the barrier was open, and most of his fellow passengers had already boarded. He trudged through carriage after carriage seeking a window seat, but eventually had to settle for a gangway one, next to a man who had occupied most of the table with his laptop and mobile phone and was already conducting a furious and frenetic series of emails and texts.

Across the gangway a mother and two rather noisy children promised to make this a less than restful seat.

He opened the paper and did his best to hide behind it.

The door from his carriage to the next, and to the doors leading to the platform, slid back and forth as more passengers crowded on. It seemed an age before the outside doors were finally slammed and the train gave a slight jerk before starting to pull out of the station. It crawled steadily through the grim north London areas, past huge blank brick walls beside the tracks sprayed with incomprehensible graffiti. The walls gave way to mile after mile of bleak residential areas studded with tower blocks and intersected by traffic clogged roads.

Tom tied to concentrate on his paper, through the jabber from his businessman neighbour, now making phone calls, and the squeals and noise from the children opposite.

Charlie Parnell arrived at The Imperial early enough to say 'Hi' to Stan, who was just leaving, and to be down in the boiler house before the plumbers had even opened their thermos flasks. He chivvied them into a promise to have the replacement pipe fitted where they had removed one from ready and usable before the matinee. 'Yes' they agreed. It would be fine. So he turned to fire up the idle boiler to start it warming in anticipation.

He was unsure about this. He had little faith in these plumbers and debated with himself about preparing the boilers for a changeover. None the less the rota that had been worked out relied on cooling the next boiler in line over the weekend so the pipework could be cut out first thing on the following Monday.

He had to start the idle boiler this early to ensure that it would have reached temperature in time to switch over for the matinee. It wasn't impossible to do this switch during the show with an audience present, but he liked to avoid it. Almost invariably a boiler change led to a fluctuation in the overall temperature of the auditorium and the backstage areas. The motorised louvres in the plenum system would immediately start to correct for any variation, but with the huge air volumes involved in a building as big as The

Imperial this correction took an noticeable length of time. The audience's comfort was always a high priority.

When he pressed the ignition button the boiler fired with a whoosh of burning jets that produced a thump which momentarily vibrated the sheet metal side panels that enclosed the weighty cast boiler itself.

He peered through the tiny spy hole that allowed him to see the burners. The flames were even and steady. The water pressures all seemed normal. Once the plumbers had fitted the replacement pipe and lagged it it only needed the stop tap valve at each end of the section to be opened and, once the circulating water had started round a brief bleed of any trapped air would have the system working again. The new section of pipe would have replaced the most calcined and restricted point in the system for that boiler, so the flow should be improved and the building's heating should be better, and cheaper. They would repeat the exercise with the other two boilers and then with other constricted parts of the plumbing.

As he left the hot, dusty and somewhat ill-lit tunnel of the boiler house the visiting plumbers were moving the new section of pipe into position where the gap from the old one yawned vacantly. Threaded flanges waited to be mated together

Back upstairs in his office Charlie idly turned over papers on his desk. Unable to settle or concentrate he went out onto his little balcony and looked across the semi lit auditorium. The iron was still in, The ad-rag hung in front of it boldly promoting the merits of local businesses. When the cloth had been new these would have been mostly big city centre department stores who could afford such exposure. Now, repainted many times by the theatre's regular sign-writer, the bulk of the space was taken by restaurants and take-aways, the latter's logos seeming inappropriately garish in that space.

He leant on the rail of his eyrie. The doors at the back of the stalls opened and a small group of cleaners came in, dragging vacuum cleaners and black rubbish sacks. They started on the long process of picking up litter from between the rows of seats and hoovering.

Charlie straightened up, brushing the pale dust from the sleeve of his black jacket. A series of distant clangs carried up the pipework rising close beside him against the proscenium wall. At least the work was under way, he thought.

With a slight sigh he went back to paperwork.

Below, in the space between the orchestra pit rail and 'A' row Paula Morley's aunt had got her vacuum cleaner lead tangled between two of the seats on 'C' row and tugged viciously and repeatedly at it. It failed to come free and cursing rather liberally she had to make her way along the rows to retrieve the flex. When she got back to the pit rail she started her daily task of getting rid of the pervasive dust.

Once she and fellow cleaners had finished The Imperial's glittering auditorium would be ready for the Friday matinee performance of "Faustus!". Carpets were clean, red velour seats were checked and brushed, opera glasses were back in their coin in the slot holders the right way up. As usual a couple of these had gone missing with the last audience and had to be replaced. In the foyer bars counters were clean, leaflet racks were tidy and restocked. The house staff would be in place, selling programmes and show merchandising and guiding the audience to its seats as the time for the matinee drew near.

As the early morning preparations were taking place Megan woke up in her digs. She'd been very lucky in this case. Frequently the owners of theatrical digs fail to accommodate the later working hours of their guests. Here Megan and the couple of other members of the company in the same digs had discovered that their preferences for late rising, and therefore late breakfasts, were not frowned on. Today Megan joined the two chorus members at the breakfast table at about ten o'clock. She ate heartily, working through cereal, bacon and egg and toast and marmalade while chatting to her colleagues. They were all very relaxed and chummy, and their landlady joined them to drink a cup of tea.

Norah Dickins, their grey haired sixty something hostess, was ever keen to indulge the preferences of the theatrical guests. Her husband, Bobby, was almost always invisible, preferring, even in the current wet weather, to hide away in the garden shed, where the conventional story was that he was working on his hobby of tinkering with old broken radios and televisions. Few of these ever became resurrected, possibly due to the major activity in the shed which in reality was studying an impressive collection of girlie magazines.

Norah got a vicarious kick out of hosting 'theatricals'. She was under no illusion that her life could ever have seen her on the boards, but she took pride in meeting and serving actors and crew. Her hard backed guest book boasted some three signatures of thespians who had gone on to become well known. In truth they had gone on to fairly minor roles in television soaps, but Norah never tired of showing visitors the appropriate pages of the book, and reminiscing about their stay with her. She believed she could recall them in vivid detail, though her recollections were probably highly coloured by whatever soap part they had each become known for.

This morning she talked to Megan and the two chorus members about a whole range of topics, but the chat came back frequently to The Imperial, and to "Faustus!". Norah was going to see "Faustus!" at the matinee that afternoon. The three guests around the table all being involved in the show meant that as usual there was no demand for an evening meal, unless you counted   Bobby, which Norah made it clear she didn't.

"I'll be back time enough to make a supper for you if you want one, and for him," she jerked her head towards the direction of the shed, "if he can drag himself away from them radio bits."
Norah probably had a fair idea what Bobby was really up to in the shed. She'd once,some years earlier, ventured into Bobby's domain with mop, duster and vacuum cleaner to sort out the mess. But she had noticeably given up this ambitious foray long before completing the self devised task. This was so unlike her usual determination to see a job through to the end that Bobby had a feeling that she'd turned up his stash. For some days after he had awaited an outburst. It never came, and their comfortable life, more a convenience than a match, continued uninterrupted.

"I hope you enjoy it."

"Oh I will, luv. I like a musical, and the songs are so good in yours aren't they? You're so lucky to hear them every day like that."

The three members of the "Faustus! company glanced at each other. As with all long running shows the company passed through periods of boredom caused by the repetitive nature of twice nightly unchanging performances. They did their work, more often than not, in a sort of auto-pilot mode. This didn't detract from the quality of their work, any more than it does with professional drivers on long journeys, if anything it ensured a continuity of standard that meant every audience got the same high class show.

"You can have too much of a good thing you know, Mrs Dickins." said John, thinking of the daily grind of his chorus part.

"Norah. You must call me Norah. Megan calls me Norah, don't you?"

"Well, as you..."

"That's right. I told you the very first time you stopped here with me, that was when you were with 'Gypsy' wasn't it, I told you, 'you must call me Norah'. And you kept on calling me Mrs Dickins, till I almost had to force you. It's so much nicer when we're all friends."

"How many times have you stopped here, Megan?" asked Keith.

"Three." she said.

"And if they were three or four week runs, that's more weeks than I spent in my own flat last year," said John.

"Well you're lucky then," said Keith, "I get fed up with staring at the four walls of mine, I spend so much time resting."

Megan mimed playing a violin in mockery at this sob story.

"I think you are all so brave, working in a profession where you might be out of work for weeks on end. I just don't know how you manage. You are all so talented, it's just unfair."

"You don't know they're talented, Norah. You haven't seen them perform yet!" joked Megan.

"Well thank you very much! Such appreciation from someone who just sits at a desk all through the show."

The two members of her chorus rose to leave. They all laughed. The breakfast chat broke up, and Norah went happily back to her house-keeping, looking forward to her theatre treat later. She prepared the lunch for Bobby and herself, and got ready the ingredients of the late supper she had promised for after the evening performance.

Chapter 11

A day in a lorry cab for Simon was not going as well as Dan had hoped. The wipers smeared back and forth across the big screen with a monotonous 'flop-flop' creating a poor view out. Each delivery point on the list today had gate security, loading bays and front office receptionists and all had to say 'hello' to Simon. Unfortunately they all tended to give him either a drink or a sweet. The result of this largesse, in particular the excess of orange juice or coke, was that the little boy's small bladder needed frequent emptying. So Dan had his normal speed of delivery, and the journey between one drop and the next, disrupted by having to seek toilets. Each of these stops involved unstrapping Simon from the passenger seat, and lifting him down from the cab. Once he was on the ground, holding his father's hand, he became even more visible, so increasing numbers of well meaning people stopped, bent down, and asked:

"Are you helping Daddy?"

Dan became conscious, and resentful, of every extra second that these well intentioned expressions of interest lost him. For the umpteenth time, he had lost count now, he lifted Simon back into the cab and sat him on the booster seat. Climbing one step up the side of the truck he could just reach the seatbelt and stretch it across his son's lap under the moulded ears on the booster that were designed to prevent it riding too high and going across the child's neck.

Simon looked down as the buckle went into the holder with an audible click.

"So you have to press that red square to get out?" the boy asked. He knew anyway, but children sometimes like to be assured that they are right.

"Yes, but don't!" answered his father, rather more sharply

than he had intended.

He walked round to the driver's side and climbed up.

"I can't reach my lorry, Dad."

The toy was on the dash board, and the child was straining against the seatbelt restraint in an attempt to grab it. His arms were too short, and he flailed his hands about, a good foot short of his aim.

Dan leaned over and passed the toy truck to his son, started the engine, and with a sharp hiss released the brakes to head towards the security gate to leave this particular drop.

He looked at his watch, then he compared it with the clock on the dashboard. They were both telling him the same thing,, that the cumulative delays would mean that the plan he had had to be finished before the tea-time rush hour started was now in tatters. Worse, he recalled, the last few deliveries were all in and around the city centre, where early evening gridlock was an unavoidable fact of life. He puzzled over changing the order of the drops, but the central ones did at least have the advantage that the firms involved were basically twenty-four hour, so he would not arrive at business gates to find them locked. He pressed the truck a little harder. The tyres sizzled on the wet roads.

The pattern of Dan's off-loadings was basically the same at each site. He would report to the loading doors, and there either the company's own fork lift truck would come to him and collect the goods, or he would use the tailgate lift and his pallet truck to off-load the lorry and bring the shipment to the customer's door, or inside.

Most of his deliveries were to the biggish companies that boasted their own fork lift and driver. This could be both a blessing and a curse for his time-table, causing him to await the truck being free, but also sometimes allowing him to leave the site while the pallets were still being shunted around the loading bay. Smaller firms involved him in un-shipping his pallet truck from its mountings and manually pushing the delivery to the doors. Nearly all his loads were small piles of goods packed onto pallets. Occasionally there would be a few heaps of loose cardboard boxes as well.

At this point, about mid-way through the delivery round, Simon was still fairly content in the cab. Soon they would have to stop for lunch. Dan would normally have eaten a sandwich at the wheel as he drove between addresses.

By mid afternoon Simon would be becoming fractious.

Sandy James was having a good day. For the first time in what seemed to him to be an eternity his heartburn had vanished as if it had never been. He wondered to himself whether it was something he had taken. He'd tried such a diverse assortment of patent digestive medicines over the past days that it would be difficult to work out which one had been effective. Then again, he wondered, what had he eaten? Or not eaten? Whatever the cause he intended to make the most of it. He started the day with his landlady's full fried breakfast, which took her slightly by surprise as she had become used to him picking at cereal, and after a leisurely morning window shopping in and out of the city's numerous bookshops he was in a café a few dozen paces from The Imperial eating pie and chips by lunchtime.

This was better. He felt well again. His might be a minor chorus part, but this afternoon, he promised himself, he would put his full concentration into it. He had no illusions. There would be no talent scout co-incidentally happening to be in the audience, who would see him and snatch him away from the humdrum to stardom. That sort of thing really didn't happen, whatever Hollywood films might imply. But he could put his best efforts into his part for this audience.

He indulged in some idle speculation about the audience. They would be, he supposed, the usual matinee mix. Mostly either older generation couples, whose retired status gave them free time in the afternoons, university students, they seemed to be in almost every audience for this show, and doubtless some school parties. He liked playing to the school parties. It appealed to a wicked streak in his sense of humour that the show drew in schools because of its link to Marlow and the playwright's current appearance on the examination reading lists, and then shocked them, or at least their accompanying teaching staff, by its raunchiness.

Sandy wasn't in the least prudish about the show's content. He was old enough to remember the way the barriers had come down in the late '60s. And in any case he was always slightly amused at the gullibility of a public that accepted at face value the suggestion of the show containing nudity. Skimpy the costumes might be, but the wardrobe comprised large quantities of flesh coloured body stockings, so that where the audience thought it was seeing flesh it almost invariably was not. Suggestive, yes. Pornographic, decidedly not.

He wiped the remaining gravy from his pie round the plate with the last chip. Through the steamed up windows and the drizzling rain outside he could see the front of a pub, and, yes, he was sure it was, John Mason going in through the doors.

'Oh well', he thought. 'if the guy wants a drink I suppose there's no reason why he shouldn't have one.' On consideration, after sitting comfortably for a few minutes, he thought he would like one too, and rising from the café table he wrapped his coat around him and made his way across the road to join the Stage Manager in the pub.

He was a little shocked when he came up to him to discover that John had clearly been drinking heavily already. Like most serious drinkers he was still upright and coherent, but his conversation had taken on the concentrated importance that accompanies the pronouncements of the inebriated.

"Sandy!" John greeted him, "Come and join me."

It had been Sandy's intention, but now it seemed to be an instruction, not a request. He clutched his half of lager, noticing that John was demolishing pints, with what seemed to be double whiskey chasers. John had managed to bag a corner table, no mean feat in a city centre pub at lunchtime, and had stocked it with several rounds at once, ready.

There had been a stranger, a local, standing by the table when Sandy approached, but he had taken the opportunity to slip away as the greetings were going on. John seemed to be almost unaware of this departure. He continued the conversation he'd been having exactly as if his audience had not changed. He was holding forth on the merits of The Imperial and buildings like it.

"The modern architects know nothing. They've got no feel. No feel. They can't build theatres to save their lives. All they're interested in in Health and Safety, bloody Health and Safety. No soul, no feel. That's what it is, no feel. Places like The Imperial they're alive, alive. They make you want to go in and enjoy yourself. Feel." he paused momentarily to take a gulp of his beer.

"Feel." he continued, "You don't get feel with modern theatres. It's all clinical, all safe, all clinical, no feel"

Sandy ventured to agree, but his opinion was unnecessary. John's pontification was under way and would be unaffected by the contributions of anyone else.

"You take a show into a proper theatre and you know the house will feel right. Right, you understand. You go into one of these modern monstrosities and it's all safety this and safety that and to hell with entertainment. They've got no feel. Now The Imperial, that's proper theatre. I first came into The Imperial thirty-five, no, I tell a lie, it was thirty-six years ago. Thirty-six years. That was 'Rocky Horror', and they had all the same fuss in the press then. But we knew. We walked onto that stage and we knew. It's got feel."

He continued in this vein for a long while, during which he worked his way through the several pints and chasers, and Sandy sipped his half.

Once Sandy saw an opportunity he jumped in with a quick "Must go." and went.

He considered what he should do. The Stage Manager's drinking was a well known thing, but should he be allowed to carry on at the rate he was going that afternoon? Sandy wondered who, if anyone to tell. If he did tell someone where John was, what could they do. Bemused he strolled along the main road and turned down to the stage door. The building was open, there were people coming and going, but they were not from the "Faustus!" company and he didn't know them. He made his way to wardrobe, an area that seemed never to sleep. As he expected the washing machines were churning, tumble driers tumbling, and wardrobe staff were ironing.

"Hello Sandy." said Susie, looking up from her iron as he came in. "How are you today?"

Despite distractions she had been keeping a careful eye on Sandy off and on ever since the night she had found him sitting alone in the dressing room as she was checking for forgotten garments. She'd spoken to him a few times, and he'd mentioned his recurrent heartburn. Today she could see he was bright and cheerful again. It had been a long time coming.

"I'm fine. Very well in fact. But I'm a bit worried about John Mason."

"Oh dear. What's happened?" like most of the company Susie was well aware of their Stage Manager's problem.

"Well it's none of my business..."

"Sandy, it's everyone's business. What's he done?"

"He's in the pub down the road. He's had a few already, and he doesn't show any sign of stopping."

"I'll have a word with Megan and Jane." promised Susie.

Relieved of responsibility Sandy made off to put his feet up, relax and read the paper.

As things turned out it was quite near to the matinee before Susie managed to see the stage management team. Her work in wardrobe kept her busy until the first noises of instrument tuning and vocal warm-ups were drifting down the show-relay speakers a little over an hour before the performance. By that time both Megan and Jane were involved in the immediate preparations for the show. They dispatched a runner to the pub to find John. But by then he had vanished. The landlord remembered him leaving about half an hour earlier. Where he had gone to remained a mystery. The only thing that was certain was that he was not in the stage management dressing room.

While Susie and Sandy were talking, below their feet, in the boiler house, the water flow was being transferred into the new section of pipe.

The two plumbers had tightened the flange joints between the new section and the old ones that bracketed it.

"What are you fannying about at?" grumbled Lloyd, the older worker.

He wiped dirty hands down the front of his already filthy overalls. He wanted to get this finished so they could go home. A long weekend beckoned. They would not be starting on the next part of the job till Monday morning, due to the matinee tomorrow. The sooner they could get out of here the more of Friday would be their own. Anything, he thought, rather than being shut down here in this rat tunnel.

What was Stephan doing? Silly ponderous sod. Always had to make everything so bloody perfect. Came of being a foreigner, Lloyd thought. He slumped down on a ledge, his overweight frame didn't deal with these hot boiler houses too well.

Stephan concentrated on turning his spanner. The spanner seemed enormous in his grip. He was skinny thin with the gaunt look of youth under the grime, but he was wiry and strong.

Again the same thing happened. He turned the spanner. He could feel the joint tightening, and then, suddenly it went slack again in his hand. Clearly the flange connection was slipping a thread, so never tightening beyond a certain point.

"Is not tighten properly." he explained.

"What do you mean it's not tightening?" demanded Lloyd, his mind running on an afternoon in the bookies.

"It goes so, then is slipped."

"Give it 'ere." and the older man lurched to his feet and took a turn at the spanner.

He had to admit the lad was right. There was a damaged

thread somewhere and repeated attempts to tighten the union beyond a certain point were in vain.

"Right then, we stop turning it just before it slips." he announced.

He realised that dealing with the problem properly would involve removing the pipe again, and fitting a new flange. There would be cutting and welding, and the time-scale was utterly impossible. His main interest was his own, but he excused himself by recalling Charlie's insistence on the timing. If the bosses want it done in a hurry, then we'll do it in a hurry, he thought

"It will be tight enough?" queried Stephan.

"Bloody soon find out when we turn the water back on."

He turned the spanner. Again he went too far and the thread slipped. He tried again. The same result. At the third go he managed to stop before the sudden loss of grip. He threw the spanner down with a clang and went to the array of wheeled valves. Swiftly he went through the process of removing the flow of one boiler and replacing it with another.

Upstairs, above the front of house, the detectors on the plenum intake fans sensed the drop in temperature as the first boiler's output was stopped. Automatically the motors engaged and shut the louvred vents to the outside world and diverted the air flow to re-cycle back into the building to avoid the auditorium cooling.

In the boiler house the first hot water started to flow through the new pipe. The system gurgled alarmingly as the water drove the air out of the section. After a few moments there was a single almighty clunk. Stephan looked over at their work cautiously. A tiny trickle of water oozed from the problem joint.

"Is leaking." announced Stephan.

"Wait a minute."

A creaking noise filled the boiler house for a few moments, to be replaced by an occasional sharp click as the new metalwork expanded.

The leak stopped.

"See mate! No problem."

Lloyd started throwing tools into his bag. They shut down the outgoing boiler, Together they left the room. Stephan looked back over his shoulder cautiously. It was all right when the water was hot. What, he wondered, would happen when the water went cold for some reason?

Upstairs the plenum system detected a return to normal temperatures in its heating matrix, and re-opened the outside louvres. The auditorium air would be both fresh and warm.

Charlie came to inspect the work a little after the two plumbers had left. He was surprised to find them gone, though relieved that he would not have to chivvy them to be done before the matinee. He could see that the new pipe was in position, and that the system was using it. He could also see that the plumbers had not replaced the lagging. Well, a few feet of exposed pipe wouldn't lose much heat down here in the sweltering boiler house. He would chase them up about that on Monday.

He made a fairly cursory inspection of the gauges, saw that the outgoing boiler was already starting to cool slightly, and flicked off the lights. He locked the boiler room door behind him. He trudged up the flights of stairs that led from the cellars towards his office in the high reaches of the building. Then stopped. He turned back and used his master key to open a door a few feet along the underground passageway from the boiler room. This room was not as hot as the one he'd just left, but it was warm, with a dry atmosphere that seemed charged with static. Inside rows of rather blank grey cabinets lined the walls, and chunky square section metal trunking was fixed in strict horizontal or vertical lines along the walls, joined at intersections or where they turned through right angles to rise through the ceiling, by steel plate corner and junction sections.

Alongside this row of cabinets big electrical breaker boxes, with eighteen inch long switch handles, were bolted to the white painted but crumbling brickwork of the walls. The breakers were on, and a gentle humming of fans filled the room.

These were the theatre's dimmers. Each conventional lantern, and all the house-lights, were supplied power from this room. The cables carrying the outputs of the dimmers snaked out of the cabinets containing the electronics, through the trunking, and up across the building to reach into almost every corner of the auditorium and stage. The dimmers were controlled by digital, so called DMX, signals from The Imperial's lighting desk at the rear of the auditorium, but, as was common with most large scale touring shows, that desk had been replaced for the run of "Faustus!" by the touring company's own.

The dimmer room was about twenty feet away from the boiler-house, and separated from it by a room used as a store. This room had been created when the dimmer room was constructed by building a brick wall across what had originally been a much bigger area. The area had always been dedicated to the business of lighting the theatre, as when the building had first been built it had housed the pipework for the, long vanished, gas lighting.

Charlie walked the length of the row of dimmer cabinets,

doing a quick visual check that all was well. Tiny LED lights glowed green at each cabinet, or rack, indicating the healthy presence of the control information required from the lighting desk. Each circuit had a red neon light next to the fuse-holder that supplied it. These red lights would come on in the event of a fuse failure, helping the instant identification of where any fault might be. None of these tell-tales were lit. Satisfied that all was superficially well Charlie turned out the light and locked the door, resuming his ascent to the upper levels.

Roughly as he was doing this Alistair was doing a similar, but more specific check of the lighting for "Faustus!". He sat at the lighting desk, which had been positioned in the auditorium for the show. Monitors glowed, showing the lighting state currently in use, and faders and keypad buttons gave him access to control the conventional lighting via the dimmers that Charlie had just checked on, the moving heads and colour changers that had come in with the show, and a variety of effects.

Alistair faded up each lantern in turn, slowly and gently to avoid the possibility of blowing the lamp by a sharp inrush of power while the lamps were still cold. He did not want to spend time getting access to and replacing the lamp in any lanterns if he could avoid it.

Satisfied that the so called generics were working and correctly positioned he went on the the movers. They all performed correctly, though he noticed a hesitancy on the part of head number twenty-three again.

"We're going to have to replace that bloody thing." he told Ben, who was loitering nearby.

"Problems?"

"That nodding bucket is draggy. I'll put the spare on instead."

"Want to do it now?"

"What's the time... Nah, we'll live with it today, I'll come in a bit early tomorrow. Can I borrow one of your crew?"

"I'll come in myself, what time do you want to start?"

They discussed the arrangements for a few moments, and Ben strolled off back down the auditorium towards the pass door humming one of the show's numbers and looking up at the rig as the movers wiggled through a series of positions in response to Alistair's continuing checking.

He made a note in the stage diary, rang Charlie in his office and told him that he would deal with the tour's request for an extra pair of hands tomorrow, and made off for a cup of tea. Strictly such assistance should have been given by the venue's electrics department, but Charlie and Ben tended to cover most minor eventualities so as to keep the wages bill down. Ben and Charlie were on fixed salaries, so no extras affected the building's expenses unexpectedly.

"Is this dodgy mover going to be all right till tomorrow?" Charlie had asked Ben during their brief phone conversation.

"He says so, You'll be the first to know if it blows up, apparently the one he's worried about is right next to your office"

"I'd better have the gaffa tape handy then." Charlie joked.

Front of house at The Imperial the first stirrings of preparations could be detected. In areas that throughout the morning had been the exclusive preserve of a couple of box office staff and the cleaners sporadic deliveries and re-stocking were in evidence. With a matinee on the way the first priority was for sweets, soft drinks and ices. The bars stood wide open with successive trolley loads of stock arriving via dedicated goods lifts from the bar cellar stores below.

Chapter 12

The two buses came into the driveway of the Thomas Lincoln School about an hour before the time arranged to leave for The Imperial. They parked in front of the main entrance, tucked nose to tail with barely more than a couple of inches between the front and rear of the vehicles. With a gentle hiss the two buses sank to their lower heights ready for boarding, and the drivers both went and sat with their feet up in the lead bus.

They were quite small buses, which was why the school had needed two for the trip. The drivers saw this as a cushy job, a couple of short runs, there and back, with a long rest, parked up in the city centre, between them. Better yet the return journey would be completed too late to be sent out on another job, but early enough in the evening to allow a night lounging in front of the television.

Edward Lovell, their boss, had been almost too keen to get this small contract from the school. Since inheriting the company from his father five years previously he had tried repeatedly to increase the use of his small business's services by local schools. His fleet provided regular transport on the daily school runs, but the occasional day trip generally seemed to go to his competitors. The number of such trips was decreasing anyway, and Edward desperately wanted to gain a major share of what little there was.

He saw such journeys, with his vehicles full of school children, as much more trouble free than contracted guided tour jobs for tour companies serving adult passengers. These, he had discovered, expected high standards of timing, service and facilities, and would complain bitterly when his company fell short of what they wanted. No-one paid any attention to any grumbles that school children might have. Accordingly he was able to cut corners on cleaning and timekeeping, cramming more trips into the daily schedule than were really possible, without penalty. A group of children arriving at school slightly late simply explained that their bus had been late, and if questioned the company could always manage to point to some specific unusual hold up, like road works or an accident to excuse the failing.

It was this thinking that had allowed John Scarings to negotiate a cheap deal for the school's visit to The Imperial.

Inside the school, amid the furious ringing of electric bells, classes of pupils were moving from one classroom to another. Amongst this tide of young people groups who were due to go to "Faustus!" split off and made their way to the hall where they had been told to gather.

In the hall they found themselves marshalled by a smiling and cheerful Nick Arthur, full of humour and with a pleasantry for almost every pupil. They found themselves disciplined and ordered about by Miss Robinson. Patsy Newbon stood aside on the fringes of the mêlée. There was no sign of John Scarings.

Untidily the pupils dropped bags on the floor and clustered into groups, chattering loudly. Miss Robinson's repeated cries of 'be quiet' were largely ignored. This was a curious situation. Pupils under the control of the teachers, but on the verge of a liberation by quitting the confines and discipline of the school and venturing out into the real world. It was exactly the potentially troublesome set of circumstances that Miss Robinson had predicted, and feared. Increasingly shrill she demanded that they stood still, kept quiet, moved into lines so she could count them and stayed where they were. Conflicting edicts poured from her mouth, and were ignored.

"Where is Mr Scarings?" she demanded of Nick Arthur at one point.

"Probably escaped to the pub for some Dutch courage if he's

got any sense" said Nick.

"He better not have done, during school hours!" Miss Robinson had no humour to speak of, and frequently failed to recognise a joke.

John arrived at exactly this moment, having checked on the buses, and collected the tickets from the secretary's office. He and Nick started the pupils moving towards the waiting transport.

There was a natural rush for the first bus. This was followed by a dive for the second bus as realisation set in that there was a chance of the back seat on that. Then within the crowd there was some jostling to be on the same bus as friends. Eventually there were too many on one bus and empty seats on the other. Instructions to move to the other bus were greeted with groans and 'but sir', but it all sorted out in the end, with Nick and a still scowling Miss Robinson in the front seat of one bus and John and Patsy in the front seat of the other.

On each bus the teachers counted heads. There was a comparison of numbers and they agreed that they had all the pupils. Doors shut. Suspensions rose again and the convoy set off for the city centre. There were cheers on board as the escapees were driven round the sweep of the drive and past the windows of classrooms still filled with captive students.

"I think they're being very rowdy." Miss Robinson told Nick.

"I think they're pleased to be escaping." he answered, "Aren't you?"

"I can't say that I'm looking forward to this scandalous production."

"I bet Marlowe's original version was a sight more bawdy

than anything we'll see today." Nick replied cheerfully.

Miss Robinson sniffed and turned towards the window. It was not too clean, and now streaked with diagonal stripes of rain in the dirt. She found that she had a sweet wrapper under her foot, and her distaste for the whole expedition continued to grow.

On the other coach Patsy sneaked a sideways glance at John. He was staring straight ahead out through the huge expanse of windscreen which was being smeared regularly by the tall wipers. The rear of the lead coach seemed very close as they drove along.

'Leave the Push and Shove. Travel with Love..ll' announced foot high lettering across the back of the other bus.

"It's not the best slogan in the world is it?" giggled Patsy.

"Have you noticed the telephone number," John asked her, "it ends 666. The mark of the devil!"

"Oh. I hope it's not an omen."

"I don't think any devils will bother us. We've got our own on board," John nodded back towards the noisy pupils behind, "they'd see off any threat in a moment."

"You don't mean that. Some of them really like you, you know."

"I know, I have to keep avoiding her."

"I didn't mean just her, but yes her too."

"She's managed to get herself on this bus you know. My very own teenage stalker."

Patsy looked back at the seats behind. Most were bent down over their mobile phones. Two rows back from where she and John sat Gemma Barrents' eyes were fixed on the back of John's head.

"Not a complication that I really want on this trip," John said, "Miss Robinson's on the look out for the slightest problem."

"I'm sure that's not really true. Anyway it'll be fine. Your stalker can't get anywhere near you in an auditorium surrounded by people."

"Well I worry about what might be said, even if it isn't true." John broke off abruptly as the bus stopped sharply at another traffic hold up.

They were getting near to the city centre now, In fact, Patsy realised, they were moving slowly and sporadically along South Parade. The bus was still half a mile from The Imperial, but already it was obvious that there was more traffic hold up than Patsy had expected for this time of day. It was the show itself, or rather the audience, that was the cause of their slow progress. The matinee performance attracted numerous coach parties, of which the Thomas Lincoln School's two buses were but a small part.

As each coach arrived at the front of the building it was able to pull in to the lay-by that ran along the front of The Imperial. There the passengers got out and went into the foyer. From a practical point of view this was a rather slow process, and the next coaches could not pull in to off-load until one of the ones ahead had left. Some parties got off their coaches onto the pavement wherever the bus got stuck, and walked along the street to the theatre. The rain that day rather discouraged this. In any case it caused nearly as much delay for coaches behind, as a bus might leave the theatre's lay-by, but a following one might not be able to pull round one that was unloading at the pavement short of the building due to the sheer pressure of other traffic.

It was a situation that was familiar to all the bus drivers. It was familiar to many of the local motorists, who avoided South Parade at known problem times of day, or evening.

John found himself looking at his watch. But they were still in plenty of time. The shop windows were lit because of the dullness of the weather, and the side windows of the school's buses glinted and sparkled with reflections on the wet glass. Because of the traffic much of the reflected light was a succession of red glares from the brake lights ahead of them.

In the lead coach Miss Robinson's mouth turned down even more than usual and she pursed her lips severely. Nick looked out at the wet streets and nearly stationary traffic cheerfully.

They each approached the theatre with different expectations, Nick of a couple of hours of entertainment, Miss Robinson of a couple of hours of over-loud misery. Miss Robinson half hoped that this interminable journey would take too long, and that they would arrive too late to be admitted to the show.

On the opposite side of the city Norah Dickins's preparations were nearly complete. All the ingredients for the supper after the evening show were carefully stored on covered plates and dishes in the fridge. A light meal was ready, with simple written instructions, for her husband. She had called to him in the shed to announce her imminent departure, and told him about his tea. As usual Bobby had accepted these instructions with a slightly distant and detached air, so she was frustrated to realise that she had no real clue as to whether the information had sunk in.

Now, with her form somewhat overdressed for a matinee performance, in a suit style dress, with her best coat and uncomfortably high heeled shoes, she was ready to leave the house.

Something held her back. She couldn't put a name to the strange feeling that she had. She was certainly looking forward to the show. She opened her handbag yet again and checked on the ticket. The piece of white card, with the logo of The Imperial printed in bold colours across it, and just below, in a gloomy black typeface "Faustus!" and the date and time, with her seat row and number below that. Across at an erratic angle a rubber stamp had been added with the single word 'Complimentary'.

Had Norah known it the show information and seat details had all been added by a printer in the box office that was fed the multi-coloured ticket blanks from a continuous zig-zag folded pile in a box on the floor below the box office counter. Thus the box office was able to produce, on demand, a specific numbered, dated ticket for any of the shows that were coming up at the venue nearly twelve months ahead. To Norah, and many like her, her ticket was not a quick solution to a complex logistical problem for the theatre, but a special passport to a few hours of pleasure. Norah anticipated the show keenly. She looked forward to spotting her current house-guests, though she realised that she would not see Megan.

Still something made her take a look round at her house as she opened the door to leave. Then briskly, as was her way, she shut the door, and made off down the street towards the bus stop on the main road.

Her ticket showed her seat as D19 in the Upper Circle. Norah didn't know it, but, despite her ticket being a 'comp', given free to her due to her accommodating some of the "Faustus!" company, it had been a help to the box office when the request for one single seat for the matinee performance had come through from the touring company manager's office.

Due to the block booking made early by The Thomas Lincoln School row D in the Upper Circle had, for weeks, exhibited a single, un-booked, seat almost exactly in the middle of the row. The request, on Megan's behalf, had enabled them to tidy up an obvious and not attractive hole in the plan, while only giving away a relatively low value seat. The box office was, in any case, obliged to, and used to, allowing some free seats for the visiting company for friends, relations, and on odd occasions important members of the production team, not on the road with the show, but visiting it to ensure that overall standards were being kept up.

The venue itself also sometimes needed to make 'comps' available, to its own directors and staff, and to the press when they wished to review a show.

None of these 'important' candidates for free seats could really have been sandwiched into the Upper Circle's D19. It had the advantage of being central, but that meant scrambling over seventeen or eighteen other patrons to get in or out of the seat, and the Upper Circle was a budget part of the house.

The Imperial did pride itself on not having any 'bad' seats. The Victorian design had ensured that every member of the audience could both see and hear with no obstructions, and the venue was known throughout the country as one of the best theatres to see any show in.

Waiting at her bus stop for the number 76 to take her to the centre of the city Norah neither knew, nor cared about any of this. She turned her collar up against the drizzle. She had considered bringing an umbrella, but had had the foresight to realise that it would be a liability in the theatre. She was a bit distressed at the way the rain was wetting and flattening her hair, making her look even greyer than usual, so she was cheered by the blurry sight of the bus approaching, its headlights reflecting off the wet road in the gathering dusk.

Waving her bus pass she climbed aboard. As most travellers were starting to try to leave the city to go home this inbound service was quite empty, and she was able to sit at the front, watching the route into the centre through the big windows at the front as the wipers cleared them.

She wondered if any of the scattering of passengers were heading for the theatre too. She would soon know when they reached the South Parade stop nearest to The Imperial.

Tom's journey towards the theatre had turned into a long drawn out series of delays. Only a few miles out of London the train had suffered a breakdown. The first indication of this had been their grinding to a halt in the middle of nowhere. Through the grimy windows there were views of wet fields. Inside, after they had been stationary for about quarter of an hour, mobile phones were out. Tom's businessman neighbour was loud and bombastic in his recounting of the hold up to the colleagues that he called. The family opposite grew rowdier and less controlled, and began running up and down the carriage, screaming.

After twenty minutes a somewhat curt apology, half indistinguishable over the noise, and due to the impenetrable accent of the rail employee making it, explained that they were awaiting a spare engine.

With the main line thus blocked the rail company dispatched an engine to the breakdown with commendable speed, but it was still a long wait for the captives until a sudden jerk, and some flickering of the internal lights gave a sign that they might be on the move again.

Any hope of making up time was shattered with the announcement, on arrival at the next station, that the next part of the delayed journey was to be by a replacement bus service.

Depressed, irritable, frustrated and delayed passengers gathered their bags and cases together and spilled out onto the platform. There was no sign of station staff, but somehow the news that the buses were on the other side of the tracks filtered through the crowd. Sullenly the stranded public climbed the steps of the footbridge across the line. Some muttered about complaint procedures, but most just hoped for luck and speed with the rest of their journey.

The front runners had boarded the buses lined up in the station yard by the time Tom came down the steps from the bridge. The choice of seats was limited again, and he was annoyed to find that the transfer had not separated him from the noisy family. They were just behind him. Was all this aggravation worth it? He had some doubt that his objective was possible. Maybe Megan would not return. He had to try though. He was cash strapped and likely to become homeless soon.

The bus convoy jerked away. They were to be taken one stop down the line to join a replacement train.

As it turned out they were taken one stop down the line to wait for a replacement train.

While they lingered on the platform Tom did, at last, succeed in finding a position among the crowd that would mean that he was away from the noisiest of his fellow passengers.

What became clear was that Tom would not be at The Imperial before the matinee started. Perhaps, he thought, he could persuade Megan to join him for tea between shows to discuss things. He realised he didn't know the running time of the show, so had no idea of how much break Megan would have between the matinee and evening performances.

He drifted off into a slightly erotic daydream in which he and Megan were reconciled and reunited in a sexual fantasy land that occupied his mind once aboard the train for many miles, until he realised that he was pressing his genitals through his trousers below the carriage table. Checking guiltily that he had not been observed he hunched forward with his hands on the table and looked at the gathering darkness outside the carriage window.

He had been travelling, or waiting to travel, all day.

The train, with the timetable severely disrupted, made slow, and sometimes erratic progress past the anonymous fields and scattered houses that spread between the towns they passed. Stations that they did not stop at appeared and vanished as a glare of cold fluorescent light, sometimes too quickly to identify the station name, but more often at a crawl that revealed unfamiliar or half recalled names, none of which were helpful to him in guessing where along the route they had reached.

Tired, frustrated and with increasing reservations about the likely outcome of his journey, Tom closed his eyes.

Chapter 13

Inside The Imperial staff and members of the company made their routine preparations.

In the box office a stack of envelopes, containing tickets for the afternoon show that had been paid for, but were awaiting collection, lay in a tray on the counter, sorted into alphabetical order. This was the best preparation that the box office could make. It was, however, a foregone conclusion that a good number of the customers collecting would slow the process, and cause queues by giving a different name to the one in which they had booked. This confusion happened frequently where a couple were not actually married, and had different surnames, or where the tickets had been ordered on behalf of someone else.

The box office tried to reduce the traffic jam that such vagueness caused by advising that reserved seats must be collected half an hour before the show was due to start. Many would ignore this instruction.

Weekday matinees generally caused additional box office queues due to a tendency for people leaving off work to call in to the theatre on the way home to book for forthcoming shows, so the staff were dealing with both the current performance, and trying to book seats for dates many months ahead. They tried to deal with this by moving at least one of the telephone bookings staff to the front counter for the busiest part of the time, but this had the effect of leaving telephone booking customers in a limbo of being told that their call was important to the theatre, and that they were third in the queue. This recording then switched automatically to a tediously repetitive jingly tune, into which periodic advertisements for forthcoming attractions were inserted.

The bars knew that pre-show alcohol sales would be low, but

that they might pick up for the interval. In general matinee audiences would be soft drink and tea and coffee consumers. Conversely the ice cream sales could be relatively high. Refreshment sales in all areas were very influenced by the particular show. Overall the "Faustus!" audiences had, for no obvious reason, proven to be spirits drinkers.

On stage a milling gathering of the cast ran through scales and exercises as part of the 'vocal warm up' that was being undertaken. If the truth were told the stage had become a noisy place in the run up to the half. Musicians were tuning instruments, and this applied to both the pit orchestra and the on-stage group. The stage crew were gently running the various motorised trucks back and forth to check their operation and positioning, and from the rear of the auditorium the sound engineer was working his way through the pile of radio mics, checking each one with a quick 'one-two' that was being fed to both the PA system, and to the on-stage foldback.

Megan walked through the midst of this apparent mayhem to the stage manager's desk. She put the prompt copy down, opened the show log book, writing the date, and performance number 253 before setting up her chess pieces. Below her, in the pit, the timpanist carefully removed the dust sheets he'd taken to covering his drums with and rolled the material in a ball which he threw to the back of the pit. He added to the general cacophony by tuning the timps. Satisfied he tried out a couple of pitch shifting blows on the pedal timps. 'Faustus' had a score that made more than average use of this slightly showy aspect of these drums, usually in conjunction with pitch blending on the keyboards among the on-stage group. As the timpanist and keyboard player were a long way apart, and couldn't see each other, they both derived some minor satisfaction from the precision with which they could blend their disparate instruments.

All of 'Faustus" musicians were highly competent. Many

were sought after as session musicians for recordings, where they would be used anonymously. Very few of the audience at the performances tonight would bother to read the long list of names, or even the small potted biographies beside passport size photographs in the programme that the principal instrumentalists sported.

The occasional friend or relative in the audience might seek out their specific acquaintance's name, but in general the players were hidden in obscurity.

This was true of most of the show's company. But the principals were a different matter. Generally granted a full, or at least half page write up in the programme, with a photograph and a listing of their past parts and successes, the major players were brought to the public's attention.

Front of house the staff were well into preparations to sell these programmes. In the foyer a small temporary counter was situated, laden with programmes and souvenirs of the show. Many of the ushers and usherettes carried an armful of programmes. There were two types of programme. The most expensive were the large format glossy ones with the full colour cover and some additional pages about the show, including photographs of scenes. Smaller, and cheaper, were the A5 sized basic programme. These contained the same basic information, and a generic article by a critic which had been syndicated to programme printers and would appear in the pages of programmes at several different theatres. In the interests of higher sales the usherettes carried the programmes with the large glossy ones stacked on top of the smaller and cheaper ones.

As the half approached, the moment some thirty-five minutes before curtain up, calm descended over the stage. The cast, and most of the musicians, left the stage. On Megan's instruction Tim flew the house tabs in, and climbed the ladder to drop the ad-rag in place in front of them.

House-lights were on, working lights were off. The stage was set.

Megan phoned through to front of house and announced 'Your house." to the front of house manager who answered.

There was a brief delay during which the auditorium was a huge empty shell, and then, one by one, the doors at various levels opened and the first members of the 'Faustus!" audience entered to be guided towards their seats by the staff.

This audience, like every other before it, entered the auditorium and looked up towards the great Victorian décor of The Imperial's roof. With the house-lights up their eyes were drawn straight to the great chandelier, and round the painted mouldings of the theatre. This awestruck gazing was usually then cut short by the urgent need to attend to finding their seat.

It was at about this point that Megan got the news that John Mason could not be found.

She was not unduly concerned from the point of view of the show. The company had become used to John's absences. But she was worried for John himself. His alcoholic binges were not rare, but it was unusual for him not to be present for a performance, even if he was in a state that made him useless for all practical purposes.

"Where the hell has he got to?" she asked out loud. Though in reality she was asking the question of herself.

"Does this happen often?" Ben was nearby in the wings.

"No, not really. He's always been here for a show before."

"You're worried aren't you?"

"Well I wouldn't want anything to have happened to him."
Megan admitted.

Outside on South Parade the Thomas Lincoln buses were
crawling along nose to tail. Pupils and staff were aware that
they were nearly at the theatre and several were standing up
reaching for coats and bags. The driver of the rear bus
suddenly braked hard. Those not sitting down staggered and
grabbed at handholds. From the front of the bus came a sharp
thump, as a man, squeezing between the two vehicles as they
were moving, bumped into the front panel of the second
vehicle.

"Stupid sod!" the driver loudly announced.

For a moment he expected the man to slump down to the
road as a result of the impact. Instead the man, who had been
struck on the shoulder by the front of the bus, turned to face
it and stared up at the driver through the high windscreen
with a look of mild surprise. They froze thus for a moment or
two, and then John Mason continued to make his unsteady
way towards the front of the theatre.

"He's drunk!" declared the driver.

"Oh, poor man. I hope he's all right." Patsy was instantly
worried. "We should go after him and ask."

"He's carried on pretty quickly," said John Scarings, "I don't
think it looks as though he's hurt."

They were trying to see through the front and side windows,
but the "Faustus!" Stage Manager had vanished around the
rear corner of the lead coach and was no longer in sight.

Moments later the school's two buses pulled in to the lay-by
in front of the theatre and there was a concerted rush towards
the door.

"Slowly, slowly" remonstrated John and Patsy.

Ahead Miss Robinson's attempts to organise her charges were more robust.

"Sit down! Wait. Did I tell you move?" the shouted litany of instructions poured from her mouth.

"You don't need to take your bags. Leave your bags on the bus."

Behind her, and a step nearer to the door, which had now opened, Nick Arthur grinned past Miss Robinson at the pupils.

"Follow Mr Arthur." she commanded.

The pupils spilled off both buses, mingling together and following Nick and Patsy into the foyer. The audience was already crowding this area. Even Miss Robinson was forced to abandon her attempt to count the pupils. Nick, confident as ever, led the way up the first of the flights of stairs that would take them towards the Upper Circle.

Some of the pupils tried to break away to buy sweets and programmes, but Miss Robinson, and John, brought up the rear, rounding most of these up as they went deeper into the building.

"They're wandering off!" Miss Robinson protested to John.

"Look we can't count them on the move." John caught a glimpse of a Thomas Lincoln uniform well away from their group at a merchandising stand, "We can count them once we've got them into the auditorium and sat down."

Reluctantly Miss Robinson had no choice but to agree.
Arriving eventually at the Upper Circle level Nick, who'd

checked where they would be sitting long ago when the tickets arrived, turned right and followed the curving corridor round the outside of the auditorium. The wide passageway sloped downhill following the line of the rake of the Upper Circle on the other side of the wall on his left. To his right doors to bars, private offices and toilets opened off.

The walls were lined with framed pictures and posters. The pictures mostly showed famous actors who at some time in the past century had appeared on The Imperial's stage. The posters ranged from yellowing letterpress Victorian playbills from the earliest days, to multicolour modern posters from recent years.

The teachers and pupils came to a clustered halt by the last door leading into the auditorium. The teachers marshalled their charges and tried to leave enough space for other members of the audience to pass. John, clutching the tickets, made his way to the front. He consulted with the usherette on the door.

They were to be seated in seats one to eighteen of three rows, B, C and D. The teachers would sit at the four corners of this block so the pupils were bracketed by their control. Nick and Miss Robinson took B18 and D18 respectively, which left John and Patsy in the gangway seats. As the pupils came in John handed each their ticket.

Gemma Barrents had watched how this was being arranged very attentively. She hung back among her peers to make sure that she was the last pupil in the row she expected John to be in. She would be sitting next to him.

Norah Dickins arrived at this door while this was going on. She could have been directed to go down either the left or right side of the house to gain her seat. As it turned out the side she had come meant that she had to work her way past all the pupils already seated in Row D. She ended up sitting next to Miss Robinson.

This little disturbance provided Gemma with the right distraction to get her hands on the ticket for D2. She could see that John Scarings was left with D1.

John, still standing in the gangway, realised what had happened. He went up to Patsy, who was also still to sit down. He caught her hand and swapped tickets with the one she held.

"What's going on?" Patsy queried.

"You'll see why when you sit down." he said, and nodded towards the near end of row D.

"Oh. I see. How did she manage to arrange that?"

"She can be very devious when she tries. Enjoy the show." said John, and he went to sit at the end of row B, next to Paula Morley.

Gemma was very frustrated.

Norah tried talking to Miss Robinson without success. Her approaches were met with somewhat stony looks and Norah concluded that the woman was busy and involved in supervising her charges. She transferred her talkative attentions to a young couple who came along the row from her left and took the seats on that side of her.

Miss Robinson was constant in her watchfulness over the pupils. The pupils themselves had divided naturally into predictable groups. The girls had mostly taken the front 'B' row, following Nick along to the centre of the house, and the boys had mostly gravitated to the 'D' row that was now bracketed by Miss Robinson and Patsy. Between these row 'C' was a mixture, including two teenage couples who had settled in, well out of reach of their teachers, and were now entwined on their tip-up seats.

Patsy, beside Gemma, made a half hearted attempt at small talk with the girl, but got only teenage monosyllabic response from the disappointed pupil.

As they sat members of the theatre front of house staff began coming and going up and down the gangways, selling programmes to those who had missed their chances in the foyers, and reminding the audience that they would not be allowed to take photographs during the show. Indeed they actively encouraged the punters to take pictures now while they had the chance. They drew attention to the décor of The Imperial, and many phones came out to photograph the great building. Many images almost immediately were uploaded onto social media.

Although she did not indulge in the photography session, indeed her little old mobile phone would have struggled in the fairly low lighting, Norah took great interest in the features that were pointed out. She admired the twisted vines, and the decorative moulded and painted cherubs, and she stared, with a certain bewildered awe, at the array of technical equipment that hung framing the ornate proscenium arch. Then she turned her attention to her programme, hunting through to find the names of the members of the company stopping with her, and proudly showing her more receptive neighbour the small lines of print.

As the house filled the temperature rose, and the plenum system in the roof spaces above the front of the house automatically opened the louvres, which happened to be shut, allowing some cool outside air into the auditorium to balance the effect of the heat generated by punters' bodies.

The house staff put all their efforts into the sales pitches. The Imperial was unusual in the ethos that the management had instilled geared to making audience members feel both welcome and wanted. Many theatres failed to do this.

Around the middle of 'B' row on the top layer of the auditorium Nick was the life and soul of a jovial, and slightly loud, discussion of the venue's style and décor involving the pupils nearest to him. Miss Robinson looked a couple of rows forward from her seat at this scene with evident disapproval. She could see Nick's arms gesticulating toward the vault of the ceiling above them.

"..and the Victorians chose to completely ignore the law of gravity with their decorations," he was saying, "so there are all these vines, which have very conveniently agreed to grow in geometric patterns..."

there was laughter from some of the pupils at this,

"..gave them a background for these indecently naked cherubs, who can float in the air with no visible means of support."

The pupils near him were looking up and craning their necks to study the theatre roof.

"It was very strange really. We have this notion of the Victorians as repressed and covered head to toe in clothing, and then they have all these nudes plastered, literally, because they're made of plaster, all over their theatres. I mean, look at that group of them over there floating about in space with their willies hanging out and not a care in the world."

The girls giggled. Nick knew that they would, and he was in all senses of the word, playing to the gallery. Several adults in seats near him laughed out loud. His antics were working as a warm-up act for the performance, and, in the Upper Circle at least, many of the audience had forgotten their miserable journey to the show through the city's crowded streets and incessant rain, and those nearest to Nick were listening to him pointing out how the plaster vines were all symbolic of a Bacchanalian orgy being conducted on the ceiling by the cherubs and their, also naked, lady companions.

Patsy watched her boisterous colleague's performance in the distance, worried about Gemma beside her, and looked at John's back a couple of rows away. He was making an ineffective attempt to point something out to little Paula she noticed. She looked behind her towards the entrance that they had come in by. Usherettes were starting to fidget with the curtains that would soon cover the doorway. A few feet further down the slope of the Upper Circle floor, and in front of where she sat, another, rather plain and uninviting doorway also had a lit exit sign above it. This one, she observed, bore the legend 'emergency exit' while the curtained one they'd used said simply 'exit'. Ever cautious she made a mental note of this.

She rested her hand on the arm of her seat, and was surprised when it moved. Because she was on the end of a row the right hand side of her seat was not connected to another chair. Like all the theatre's seats it was formed by two vertical cast iron frames. In the middles of rows each frame had a pair of pins sticking out, one either side, to support the seat pad, which then could tip-up using these pins as pivots. Her end seat had a normal frame between her and the next seat, Gemma's, but a single sided frame to make the end of the row. This single sided cast iron frame had been made with a vine pattern on its outside face to match the auditorium décor. It had a single pin, supporting just that side of her seat. At the top of the frame a flat cast plate formed part of the metalwork, and supported the arm, which was a simple wooden block, padded and covered with the red velour that upholstered the auditorium. To her left the shared arm adjacent to Gemma's seat was solid and firm. On Patsy's right the arm wobbled.

With her mechanical interest piqued she began to explore the fixing of this arm. She soon discovered that it was simple in the extreme, consisting of nothing more that a couple of wood screws passing up through the cast plate and screwed into the wood of the arm.

"Ow!" she exclaimed, as she found that these screws were not only loose in the casting, which had worn over a century where the steel screws passed through, but that the heads were also razor sharp. This had happened due to maintenance repeatedly tightening the screws in the increasingly worn wood of the arm, and on several occasions having the screwdriver slip as they tried the contortionist challenge of tightening an upward facing screw in an inconvenient position.

Patsy determined not to poke about with the seat's fixings any more and settled back to await the start of the show.

In the house manager's office on the ground floor a small incident was having to be resolved.

After his minor collision with the Thomas Lincoln School bus John Mason had arrived at the pavement outside the theatre. In error he had turned left, and ended up going down the mean alleyway on that side of the building, which was designed to provide an escape route from the exit doors that served the OP side. As he moved up and down the alley he was confronted by blank brick walls and the occasional double exit door. These exits had no means of opening them from the outside, and were secured inside by panic bars, an assembly that forced vertical bolt rods into the top and bottom of the frame to lock the door, but included horizontal bars that operated a lever to release the bolts if the bar was pushed. These antique fixings were a simple mechanical means of ensuring that the doors would open if a crush of patrons were to be forced against them in case of a need to escape. They would not open from the outside for John Mason, or anyone else.

He knocked on a couple of these doors in his drunken haze, but no-one heard, as each door was at the bottom of a concrete stairway coming from the Dress or Upper Circle, or in the case of the stalls escape at the end of a drab concrete passageway.

He stepped back to look up at the sheer blankness of the theatre's side wall. It rose high above him, and as he stepped back to take it in he bumped into the wall of the adjacent building. Leaning against that he scanned the roof-line, and it dawned on him that the recognisable rectangular block of the fly tower was to his left. Drunk he might have been, but theatre instinct engrained from years in the industry immediately told him that he was on the OP side, and he remembered that The Imperial's stage door was on its prompt side. He set off on a staggering journey to make for the stage door. To do so he passed the front of house, and, partly swept up by the audience pouring into the building for the performance, and partly because he identified it as a way in, he turned into the foyer.

The House Manager was very quick. He recognised John instantly, and he also identified the problem. John's drinking was an open secret, but he'd not been seen like this for a long while. The House Manager had him by an arm and had led him into his office before almost anyone in the foyer was aware of his presence.

Once there John found himself seated on a chair, hearing instructions being issued to the manager's secretary for black coffee.

Backstage Megan was slightly surprised when the phone over the stage manager's desk rang. It was actually mere chance that she was at the desk. Show running was such a routine that she normally stayed in the stage management dressing room after she had called the half, except for brief visits to stage for any details that needed sorting out, and for the quarter and the five minute calls. As it happened she was chatting to her chess opponent over the talk-back system.

"Hello?"

"Front of house here. We've got something here in the office that belongs to you."

Megan had a flash of inspiration and guessed.

"Is he sober?"

"As a newt," came the reply. "I think I'd better keep him in my office for the moment while we get the house in. I've ordered up some coffee. Perhaps we'll see what he's like at the interval."

"Thank you. I'm really sorry."

"Don't worry about it. As long as he doesn't throw up on my office carpet."

So the show would start with John tucked safely away in the house manager's office. Megan had no qualms about the performance without him. His role was more administrative than practical, and the touring crew knew the show inside out. She did wonder what had caused this relapse. No-one could have pretended that John had stopped drinking, but it was highly unusual for him to be rendered incapable. She couldn't remember when she'd last seen him in that state. She debated about making a note in the stage log book, and decided against it. She could always add it as a footnote if there was any problem with this performance. Other than that she preferred not to reveal the situation to the production company. No-one in the production company office would know, provided they didn't happen to ring and ask for him for the next few hours. If they did she could always say he was busy and would ring them back. The "Faustus!" company would take care of its own.

"Ladies and gentlemen this is your quarter hour call. Fifteen minutes please." Megan said into the microphone.

She looked at the clock above the desk. In truth the phone call from front of house had made her a few seconds late with this call. It was only really about eighteen minutes to curtain up. She had a certain private pride in giving the calls with second perfect precision. Slightly superstitiously she hoped that the late call wasn't an omen.

She looked over her shoulder at Jane, who was nearby in the wings talking to Ben. Should she worry about her talking to Ben, Megan wondered with a pang of jealousy. No, that was silly. Jane wasn't the type to muscle in on whatever tentative relationship might be starting between Ben and herself, however much she fancied him. And it was clear that she did. She had said so, and the body language now, in the gloom of the wings, left no doubt. At least, Megan rationalised, it left no doubt to her, but Ben seemed completely unaware of the signals Jane was sending. Maybe Jane didn't even know she was doing it Megan thought.

"They've found John." she told them.

"Where is he?" asked Jane, instantly abandoning her half-hearted chatting up of Ben.

"In the FOH Manager's office."

"Drunk?"

"I'm afraid so. They're going to look after him for the first half."

"Shall I go round and get him?" Jane offered.

"No, I think we'll leave him there for the moment. You can't watch him while the show's running."
As it turned out it was a wise choice, since by the time Megan and Jane were having this conversation John was already asleep, slumped in the house manager's office chair under the slightly disapproving and watchful eye of the secretary, who had returned with the coffee to find him already asleep.

Above Megan's head Tim climbed the ladder to start flying the ad-rag out.

Many of the audience, including Patsy, noticed the ad-rag rising, and watched as it slipped upwards into the concealed slot between the auditorium ceiling and the proscenium arch. Patsy was fascinated by this, pondering, with a mind trained from childhood by her father to look at how things worked, the mechanics of what she could see. Because she was watching so closely she was perhaps the only member of the audience to see the faint, almost undetectable, haze high up on her side of the stage that followed the advertising's disappearance.

She would have liked to point this curious effect out to someone, but Gemma beside her seemed unreceptive to small talk. She wondered if John had seen it too, but he was too far in front of her for any certainty as to which way he was looking.

From the Dress and Upper Circles, each nine rows deep, the audience could now see the members of the orchestra making their way into the pit. Customers on the ground floor in the stalls were less aware of the arrivals, especially if they were seated towards the rear. The sight-lines from every seat in the

Victorian design gave excellent views of the stage, but were not intended to let you see the orchestra.

It was in the Circles therefore that the first gentle stirrings of expectation among the public could be felt. Alistair settled himself behind the lighting desk.

Megan announced:
"Ladies and gentlemen this is your five minute call, five minutes please."

She grinned. Better. Smack on time.

Front of house the usherettes passed the public into the house a bit faster. As usual many customers were arriving in the last few minutes. This was where the slick machine of the theatre came into its own, hastening, without seeming to hurry, its more tardy guests.

In the Upper Circle the latecomers on 'A' row, in front of the Thomas Lincoln School, included several pensioner couples and a family group of mother, father and two quite young children. The children looked around excitedly, jumped to their feet after sitting down, and leant over the front rail to look down onto the Dress Circle and Stalls below.

Miss Robinson watched the children's antics grumpily. She would have liked to impose some discipline. Her belief in children sitting quietly and behaving extended to what she expected of them in a theatre too. She felt that the earliest possible familiarity with sitting, watching and concentrating was best. The loose chaos of pantomime was an anathema to her and she thought of the wriggling and squirming that was being displayed as bad behaviour.

She also doubted that this production was suitable for these children who were, what were they, perhaps seven or eight years old. They would, she decided, not appreciate the meaning and background to the original play, and she was certain that this musical version was not a good introduction to it for them.

She failed to acknowledge the enormous popularist following that "Faustus!" had achieved. To her it was a corrupted version of a classic text. She hardly even thought of Marlowe's original as a play for performance. She was not open to the possibility of the text forming the basis of something that was specifically designed to be entertainment. Her blinkered thinking of theatre as an 'art' form and this play as a literary work, not entertainment, did not allow her to perceive that good shows are devised to be enjoyed at a variety of different levels. The creators of "Faustus!" had been shrewd in weaving the well known storyline into successful popular music and creative visual effects in a way that gave it popular box office appeal to a range of audiences. They were reaping the financial rewards for their abilities, and the public was being treated to entertainment at its best.

Throughout the great foyer and bars speakers gently urged:

"Take your seats now please ladies and gentlemen, this afternoon's performance will commence in five minutes."

Backstage Megan's voice found its way into dressing rooms, the green room, corridors and the wardrobe:

"Ladies and gentlemen this is your beginners call. Act one beginners please. Mr Marsden and members of the chorus this is your call."

Five minutes to go.

In the House Manager's office John Mason slumbered.

Charlie Parnell came out onto his office balcony. He looked down at the sea of heads in the stalls below, and to his left towards the two circles, where he could see faces. Faces looking about, faces buried in programmes and faces turned towards each other talking. The auditorium appeared as a patchwork of colours, with more splashes of red than you'd expect, but here and there a large block of a single colour betrayed the presence of a school party. He could see one such chunk of blue close to him on his side of the Upper Circle level. This was the Thomas Lincoln party. In front of them he could see some small children climbing up the handrail to look over the edge. He wasn't concerned that they might fall over, but he did wonder if the parents would sit them down when the show started.

Despite his best intentions there were still parts of "Faustus!" that Charlie had not yet seen, so he had decided to watch this matinee from his office balcony. It was not the best view of the show, but he shuffled to a place where the worst of the obstructions caused by lighting gear and cabling were out of his way. Having found the most suitable place he leant on the rail.

"Take your seats now please. This afternoon's performance will commence in two minutes."

On stage the cast were in position. Out front the sound engineer idly eavesdropped occasional backstage conversations via the radio mics over his headphones. Rarely he would happen upon interesting exchanges revealing who was sleeping with whom. Mostly the cast conversations were very mundane. This performance was no exception. The ushers and usherettes were shutting the last doors and closing the blackout curtains over them. Final reminders to the audience that photography and recording were not permitted and to turn off mobile phones were given.

Megan looked at her row of monitors, concentrating on the one that showed her the conductor. For a moment there was no sign of him, but suddenly he appeared, rising up from the bottom of the frame, having been bent down fiddling with something below her field of view. As usual he looked straight at the camera and winked. Simultaneously the phone rang. Megan picked up the receiver.

"Stage."

"You have front of house clearance." came the rather formal permission from the house manager.

"Thanks. How's your guest?"

"Asleep in my office. Talk to you later." and there was the click of the line going dead.

Megan gave her standbys, and moments later the overture struck up. A full house of theatregoers tapped its feet and settled in to enjoy the show, recognising the parts of the introduction that were the more famous, familiar hit numbers from the show.

It was a matinee, so this afternoon's rendition didn't quite get the audience clapping along to the up-tempo parts, but some foot stamping could be heard at various points.

The house-lights faded and the audience's eyes became fixed on the roseate glow of the light warming the main tabs.

A keen observer might have just seen the slightest movement of the curtains as Tim took the brake off the front of house tabs hauling rope.

Megan wrote the 'time up' on the page for performance 253 of the show log. They were exactly on time. She smiled to herself with satisfaction.

Chapter 14

One of the voices that the operator had eavesdropped from his sound desk had been that of Penny Abbott, in her dressing room, squeezed into her flesh coloured body suit and already fitted with her radio mic, with the transmitter discreetly concealed, and the mic taped up through her blonde hair to her forehead. Wrapped in her dressing gown in front of the mirror she let rip with a series of vocal warbles as she ran up and down the scales.

Susie knocked on the door and came in carrying Penny's Act two costume which had been having a last minute press.

The overture could be heard via the show relay speaker over the dressing table. There was no hurry. Helen's first appearance was not till well into the show, at the end of the first act.

"Here you are Penny."

"Thank you Susie. How are you today?"

"I'm fine. And it's another full house, as if I needed to tell you that."

"It's always nice to be re-assured. The usual mixture?"

"Yes, but there's a couple of school parties up in the gods, and it looked as though there were a lot of OAPs"

"Dear god! Two sorts of people to offend. Maybe I should invest in a bigger fig leaf!"

They laughed. It was all very relaxed. The company was going through the performances on a kind of comfortable auto-pilot.

"Hard at work?" Susie asked with a nod at the laptop on the dressing table.

"Proofs of my last photo shoot."

"I daren't ask to see those. I'm too innocent and young for those sorts of pictures." Susie said.

"I bet you aren't. I bet you're one of those girls who takes pictures of themselves in their bedroom mirror and posts them all over the internet."

"I am not!" Susie protested. Then she saw the grin on Penny's face and realised her leg was being pulled.

"Well you should. You'd get a huge following."

"Oh you! I never know when you're joking." and she left.

Brian Marsden perched on the bench behind the book strewn table under the overhang of the rostrum that supported the on-stage group. Not for the first time he muttered a silent curse at the inadequate width and hardness of this perch. Like so much scenic furniture the design was done to fit available spaces and visual requirements rather than the comfort of the cast. This bench was sandwiched tightly upstage of the table and had been made as narrow as possible so that he could get in and out without knocking the scenic wall behind or the table in front. Some of the pile of oversized books on the table overhung the edge. He would have moved them long ago, but they were fixed to the table top so that they could not fall off during scene changes. Their positioning was artistic, but inconvenient.

The overture ended to applause, and the tabs rose to the opening bars of 'Always Working' as the chorus simultaneously criss crossed the stage and launched into the first number.

From the auditorium the public immediately saw a swirling mass of medieval costumes, was assaulted by the raucousness of the number, which was delivered by the chorus in their roles as common townsfolk, and saw this seeming crowd of humanity part with choreographed precision to reveal Brian, as Faustus, seated in his supposed study, deep in his books.

In response to Megan's cues the wide, full stage, lighting brightened on Brian and his study and gradually dimmed across the rest of the stage as the number wound to a close and the chorus gradually left the scene.

The audience applauded the end of the number. Actually there'd always been some friendly banter backstage between Brian and the chorus about whether this particular round of applause was for their performance, or in recognition of his first appearance. Brian argued that the applause was their traditional welcoming of the star's first entrance.

The Thomas Lincoln party watched, like the rest of the audience, with rapt attention. Miss Robinson watched, at first with her pre-determined distaste, and then with a growing though grudging admiration for the way that the writers had incorporated the feel, the sense, and even in part the Marlowe script into this opening scene. Reluctantly she admitted to herself that, though she despised the musical format, and hated the particular style of this show, she was not as utterly opposed as she had been. She was reactionary in her views, but mature enough for grudging acceptance of some of what was being put before her so far. Her attitude could change.

Nick was, frankly enthralled by the vibrant energy of the company ensemble. Wishing to himself that he could force half the pace and verve out of his pupils when he directed the school shows as this professional company had. He was aware in the back of his mind that many of the cast were miked up, none the less he felt a surge of resentment that this company could burst out over the musical level of the orchestra he could see in the pit. He was unaware yet of the rock band style element which was to come from the on-stage group. His memories were of the endless fights with the head of music at the school during which he begged, pleaded and even threatened in his efforts to reduce the sound level from any orchestra dragged together for a school musical show. He regretted the wasted effort. Nothing, it seemed, would ever persuade the music department to play more quietly, so the carefully rehearsed lyrics of his singers were always lost below the bellow of sound from the instrumentalists. Wasted hours hanging curtains along the front of band enclosures to try to deaden the noise sprang to mind. If only... he thought.

John was pleased with what he was seeing. He genuinely believed that this would bring the dusty text they were studying to life for his pupils. Looking about he could see the bulk of his charges were intent on the performance. Paula Morley, dwarfed by the theatre tip-up seat to the extent that if she sat towards the back of the chair it threatened to fold up with her inside it, was, however, staring at the stage with the lack of reaction the characterised most of her school hours.

Patsy was beginning to relax. Much as she loved the theatre her infrequent visits due to her loneliness had not yet made her immune to the initial dwarfing effect of The Imperial's grandiloquence. It did seem to her though that her fears of risqué or even pornographic content were going to be unfounded. Perhaps the press had exaggerated. Maybe she would not need to face the classes next week, red faced in the knowledge that she had taken them to see nudity, and worse, that they knew that she had been watching what they had seen too. She too could detect a spirit of concentration among the school party that she, at least, had never been able to achieve with them in the classroom. Even Gemma Barrents, beside her, was, Patsy decided, slipping out of her previous sulk and starting to enjoy the performance for its own sake.

It was true. Gemma had, if not forgotten, at least pushed John Scarings to the back of her mind. Realistically she knew that her fantasy of a romantic tryst in the midst of her classmates had been too optimistic. She saw her peers as juvenile and silly, lacking her maturity. They would nudge and giggle. She yearned for gentle groping with the object of her affection, but not to become a spectator sport for the year group.

The two entwined couples somewhere around the centre of the three rows of seating that made up the party were not so self conscious about their activities, and were both engaged in rather more than hand holding under cover of the darkness offered by the house-lights having gone down. They had stopped kissing when the show started, but hands were still busy. With a strange blinkered acceptance the other pupils chose to ignore these goings on in their midst. Miss Robinson, in the back row of their section, had been highly aware of their activities, but unable to reach the culprits, much as she would have liked to knock their heads together.

The majority of the school pupils had approached this outing with a dutiful reluctance. Now the show was under way they were seized by the action. The spectacle, though barely started, attracted them, and the music appealed. This was popular music, with a heavy emphasis on rock and pop, even though so far only played by a conventional orchestra. They'd recognised bits of the overture, and though 'Always Working' was not known outside the circle of past patrons of the show, it was in the style. Better yet this musical contained none of the recitative and sung-through semi operatic content that had blighted the theatre industry's musical output in recent years. The pupils didn't analyse the show like this. They just knew what they liked. At the moment they liked "Faustus!".

The trip was going to be a success. They were being

entertained and the teachers were accepting it as part of the educational process despite that.

The small children in 'A' row of the Upper Circle had got up again when the applause started, but their parents had dragged them back from the handrail and sat them down. There was a slight hiatus while the parents re-arranged themselves and their children so that the youngsters were between Mum and Dad and easier to restrain. Eager young eyes looked at the parents, and them straight back to the stage.

Norah was also enjoying herself. She had had to restrain herself from grabbing the arm of her new found friend in the next seat and pointing out one of her guests when she spotted him in the opening number. Her clapping as the song finished had been as loud as anyone else's. Now she was turning her attention to trying to see the other lodger, who she knew must be there in the big choral numbers. She dipped once again into her bag of mint imperials, bought in the foyer, sold with slightly wry humour by the venue in their own bespoke packaging under the simple name 'Imperials', and concentrated. But this number was going to be a solo she could tell. There was Brian Marsden, in the main role, brightly lit behind a table covered with huge books. He was about to sing.

Norah tried to remember what she had read about him in her weekly magazines' entertainment gossip columns. She'd skipped over the glowing potted biography in the programme, and now it was too dark for her to try to find the piece and read it. She would have a look during the interval, if she remembered. For now she sucked, and then crunched the mint and waited as the orchestra played the opening introductory bars of what promised to be a slower number than the last.

Norah wondered vaguely what Megan was doing. She had

little idea of the actual duties of a backstage crew during a performance. Strangely she half envisaged Megan in some sort of luxury business office, in a huge black swivel chair behind a leather topped desk answering telephones and issuing instructions.

Megan was issuing instructions, but from a much less salubrious 'office' than that in Norah's imagination. She was demonstrating her multi-tasking abilities to the full. The show cueing was proceeding with its customary slick efficiency. At the same time she was just starting her latest chess match. Physically there was a small, un-remarked, struggle taking place above the stage manager's desk.

A few nights previously there'd been a comment that some stray light was leaking onto stage during a black out from the working light above the desk. A piece of blue gel, plastic sheet used to colour stage lighting, had been found and wrapped into a cone around the offending light fitting and secured by a scrap of gaffa tape. This afternoon the heat of the bulb had finally got the better of the gaffa tape and the gel had unwound and dropped onto Megan's script. As she cued the start of Brian's first number she was refitting this improvised lamp-shade with new tape. At the same time she told her chess opponent

"Pawn to E4." a fairly conventional opening that required no attention on her part.

Sandy James bounded up the uncarpeted concrete stairs to the second floor mens' chorus dressing rooms two steps at a time. He grabbed the steel, scaffolding pipe type bannisters bracketed to the bare brick walls to give himself an extra pull up at each pace. He felt full of energy. He felt better than he had felt for a long time. He was rushing keenly to his costume change ready for his next scene.

No-one commented on his rediscovered joie de vivre in the

muggy, crowded dressing room, where half a dozen medieval citizens were transforming themselves into assorted hellish apparitions and devils. Bare light-bulbs blazed around mirrors and there was continuous chatter and the scrape of coat-hangers on metal hanging rails in the underarm deodorant scented air, competing for sound level with the show relay speaker on which Dr. Faustus' own first number could be heard starting.

The musical introduction underscored a few lines of dialogue, originally scripted by Marlowe to the 'Chorus', as Brian came down centre, tracked by the beams of the moving heads in the rig to start to sing.

"What use is science" was a slow number after the show's opener, but built to a crescendo as it went on.

It failed to appeal to the school pupils. They didn't see Brian as any sort of idol, though he had a strong following among more mature ladies, and the number's lyric was hung around Marlowe's script which the school had flogged its way through for far too many hours already.

Norah liked it. She had succumbed to the temptation and put a coin in the slot of the clamp between the two seats ahead of her to free the little pair of red plastic binoculars, and was able to study Brian's face more closely.

The Thomas Lincoln party was reverting to teenage norm, with a large proportion of them becoming sullen, with that long suffering superior and sulky air that the age group can adopt. They demonstrated their short attention span by this.

"Knight to F3" Megan responded as the number carried on, and was immediately told "Pawn to D5"

Megan made a backstage call for members of the chorus for "All Humans Sin" and put lighting and stage on standby for the impending segue into that song before she said:

"Pawn to D4".

Brian was reaching the end of his song. Norah could see, through her opera glasses, that he was sweating with the effort of the challenging solo. She made a mental note to clap loudly when it finished. The lighting sequence that was plotted around the number's end included a spreading from the tight concentration of beams that he had been in. The moving heads, obedient to the lighting desk's demands, swung outwards and downwards to cover more of the stage. Head number twenty-three squeaked as it moved. Charlie looked up and across to it. It wobbled slightly as it finished its move, and the pool of light it was creating on stage wobbled too.

Alistair cursed under his breath. His decision to postpone the replacement might not have been too wise he decided with hindsight. Too late now though, and there wouldn't be time between the matinee and evening performances.

Cast members were arriving in the wings ready. The members of the on stage group readied their instruments for the first time in this performance. "Faustus!" was about to take one of the jumps in style that happened occasionally during the score. As Brian briefly acknowledged his applause the pit orchestra played on, being joined, as the melody changed, by the electric instruments on the platform upstage. Guitars, synthesiser and drum kit came to the fore in the mix. Motorised faders on the sound desk changed positions to accommodate the new instrumentation. The moving lights began a choreographed sequence, set to mirror and mimic the dancers who had entered with the singers. Colours changed. Patterns created by the gobos inside the lanterns swept through the smoke that was being pumped into the atmosphere.

The show transformed into a rock opera, gaining the appearance of a pop video, as the dancers gyrated in the three dimensional space made by light beams striking through smoke and out into the house.

The beat produced a visceral response in the listeners. Even the older members of the audience were driven to involuntary foot tapping. The youngsters roused from the slight apathy of the previous few minutes. They had probably not heard the number unless in its brief representation in the overture, as it had not made playlists. They heard it now, and it was only the song's position, early in the show, that meant that audiences did not whistle it as they left the show.

Charlie admired the precision of the choreography and the cynical formulaic public pleasing writing of the number. He looked at the noisy moving head near him again. Wondering if it was distracting the audience he sneaked a look around the edge of his private space to the box that separated him from the corner of the Upper Circle. The box was occupied by a family. They were glued to the show and gave no sign of having heard the intrusive noise. Relieved he turned back to the stage.

Ben appeared in the prompt side wing behind Megan. He was prowling on an unplanned route checking and double checking that all was well as the show ran and the crew dealt with the occasional changes. Some saw this sort of attention to the job as obsessive, but it was a dedicated care that he shared with Charlie., The first major scenic change was due shortly. Trucks would move to new positions and Tim and his part-time casual assistant would fly a couple of pieces into view.

Megan's chess would be interrupted for a while as the touring crew, resident crew and cast all had to concentrate on the first of the complicated sequences of this performance. The company could, and frequently did, do whole sections without conscious thought. For the moment they all needed to pay attention. All except John Mason slumbering in the Front of House Manager's office with his head on one side and his mouth open, dribbling slightly.

While the scene change was happening Penny sat alone in her star room with a dressing gown slung around her shoulders studying the proofs from a recent photo shoot on the screen of her laptop. It had been a glamour shoot, bordering on the soft pornography world, and she looked with some pride at the sexy poses she had struck just a couple of days ago for the photographer. The screen showed her almost nude, thrusting her pert bottom towards the camera while the string of her thong vanished between her bum cheeks. In shots where she faced the camera she was seen lifting her breasts in their tiny bra cups by putting her arms up or her hands into her loose flowing hair. She remembered with amusement that her nipples had kept slipping into view. In some shots she was spread with her pelvis lifted toward the lens so it took no great imagination to visualise her pubis through the tiny triangle of sheer material that almost failed to cover her. Brian will appreciate these when they are published, she thought. Her mind wandered to all the other red-blooded males who might also appreciate them. And to all the women's libbers who would vilify her for posing for them. She fidgeted with the three star shaped padded overlays attached to her body stocking in the obvious strategic places.

Apart from the body stocking, which careful colour matching and the lights would render invisible once she was on the stage, these three stars would be her only covering once her cloak was raised. Her appearance in "Faustus!" might be as obscene, if not more so, since she would be dancing as she sang, as the photographs on her screen.

She wriggled and tried to shift her little concealments into more comfortable positions. The padded star at her groin was particularly uncomfortable this afternoon. Its points tended to dig into the very top of the inside of her thighs when she sat.

Knowing that this matinee audience included some school parties she fully expected the odd wolf whistle, or even lewd shouted comment, on her first appearance. Fully adult audiences were notably more restrained, though, she was assured by both managements and the fan mail, very appreciative. When the tour had started she had been unsure how to handle the ogling, the attention. She had sought the advice of some of the girls at a strip club in that first city.

"Don't look at the bastards."

"Think of the money"

"Remember you're the one in control."

"You've got it girl, so flaunt it."

advised the girls.

It was, Penny thought, really the rise of her modelling career that had given her the confidence for her nightly display. The realisation that she had not just the vocal and acting talent to gain this coveted lead part, and the musical hit coverage that came with it, but also the looks to be able to guarantee an continuing demand for her time long after "Faustus!" eventually finished, whenever that day might come.

She knew that Brian, and the rest of the cast, were revelling in the show's success. She knew too that they all secretly worried about their futures after the run. Penny, meanwhile, was assured by her agent of a landslide of offers. Some she and the agent were rejecting out of hand. The more pornographic of these, two proposals for 'films', were clearly well beyond the pale. But on the plus side she had offers for shows, recording work and television appearances ranging from a breakfast show anchor to quiz show hostess. Provided they could keep the offers waiting without losing them till the musical's run ended her future was rosy. She was in a star dressing room, with carpets and wallpaper, instead of emulsion painted walls, and had, if not the exclusive attentions of a dresser, at least considerable help from the pleasant and uncomplaining Susie. All of this, she reminded herself, added to the extra salary she was drawing, the money from recordings on which she featured and the public attention, just for showing a bit of leg. Well, quite a lot of leg really she thought.

She could hear from the show relay that her entrance was drawing closer. Megan would be calling her soon.

She scrolled through her pictures again with narcissistic pride. Yes, she thought, that was a good shot. The enigmatic smile, slightly reminiscent of the Mona Lisa, took on a whole new meaning coupled with that pose. She trusted that her agent would select which pictures to release where with care.

Reluctantly she shut down her laptop and closed its lid.

Chapter 15

Penny's appearance was the visual highlight of act one. Every member of the audience would have agreed. The male half of the public would have agreed for all the reasons that were to be expected. The female half had to agree too because the show's designers had excelled at this point, and to have excelled in a show with such a glut of great moments was to be among the all time greats of live theatre.

As the company approached the interval, having sung, danced and played their way through the great set-piece 'Black and White' number which used monochromatic costumes and lighting in a bewildering criss cross pattern, choreographed so that it was almost impossible to follow the individual identity of any one dancer, Megan called Penny and the rest of the company for the Act one finale.

She'd advanced her chess game somewhat in the slacker moments, and her pieces were threatening on her opponent's king.

As Brian played a small, music free scene downstage in front of a trucked scenic item the crew were positioning the motorised parts of the grand reveal for 'Helen of Troy'. A huge staircase centre stage was concealed from the audience by two of the motorised trucks, which were set to pivot outwards to display Penny in the role at the appropriate moment. The hidden, upstage, sides of these trucks contained giant industrial fans and a couple of smoke guns.

Penny came from her dressing room along the passageway to the stage. She took her dressing gown off as she reached the bottom of her staircase, threw it to Susie, and climbed up to the twelfth step. High above, on instructions from Megan, Tim gently flew in the huge flimsy cloak which was positioned so its false shoulder pads seemed to sit on her. Stage hands gently stretched the material out so it spread evenly from her shoulders to a wide arc on the stage floor some ten or eleven feet below her feet. The trucks swung shut enclosing her ready.

Brian concluded his speech, and conjured up Frank Durban to demand he show him Helen of Troy. The music for 'Make Me Immortal' began. Keening electric guitars from the group, and that familiar bass beat on the two pedal tymps.

There did seem to be a lot of dust again the percussionist thought.

The audience tensed noticeably. They knew this number. They knew what must be about to happen.

Lighting changed towards the motorised trucks, which swung open in a blaze of amber light revealing a figure, clad in a twenty foot long gown perched high up in the centre of the stage.

The smoke guns had fired, and the scene was a solid mass of swirling lit cloud.

Megan called cues at speed.

The huge fans started to turn. Initially the smoke cleared away from Penny, giving the auditorium its first proper glimpse of her. Then, as they came up to speed the wind caught the material of her gown and spread it upwards and outwards, till she stood, seemingly naked but for her three little stars, atop a staircase while her gown filled the whole width of the stage in a giant rippling semi-circle of golden material.

Penny's hair blew out in a halo around her head, and as the gown was flown away into the grid she descended the staircase with Brian, and the chorus singing 'Make Me Immortal'.

The sound level of the song drowned out the murmur of lustful appreciation from the boys of the Thomas Lincoln party. Miss Robinson scowled her disapproval, at the boys, at the song, at the provocative display.

As the number concluded Penny stood against Brian with her arms stretched straight over his shoulders and crossed behind his head as they kissed and the lighting snapped to blackout and the tabs fell to the usual thunderous applause and a half standing ovation.

Brian squeezed Penny's bottom as the working lights came on. She smacked his hand away half heartedly.

"It's called 'make me immortal', not 'make me immoral'." she joked, taking her dressing gown from Susie and slipping it on.

"I prefer immoral" said Brian.

"Yes. So we've all heard. Anyway certainly not here." said Penny, leaving the proposition slightly open.

"We could ask for a longer interval." Brian suggested, and they made off towards the dressing rooms arm in arm laughing.

The house-lights came up in the auditorium. The ushers drew back the curtains over the doors, and swung them open. The ice cream trolleys appeared. Tip up seats thumped as the audience not already on its feet rose and stretched. There was a general scrambling for the ice cream queue and towards the bars and the toilets.

Three of Thomas Lincoln's fifteen year old boys tried to buy beer from the Upper Circle bar, and were politely, but firmly refused. The bar staff grinned at each other as the boys turned away. It was a common school party attempt. The culprits never seemed to realise what a give-away a school uniform was.

All theatres are stretched to the limits by an interval. Sales outlets of all sorts serve at breakneck speed, but it is the plumbing that takes the most hammering. For a fifteen minute period the repeated flushings and running of taps were stretching The Imperial's aged systems. One immediate result was the draining of gallons of hot water from the system. The same boilers that provided the building's heat fed the hot water tanks. Now the temperature of those tanks dropped dramatically, and the boilers cut in to restore the hot water.

In the boiler house the vibration of the roaring boilers began shaking the new pipework with the recently made suspect joint.

A small drip emerged from the threaded union. Boiling water oozed out, and evaporated almost immediately. Gradually the tiny weeping became more, till by the end of the interval a minor trickle was running out just faster than it could steam off, and a small puddle began to form on the bare concrete floor. The boiler house atmosphere changed from hot, to hot and steamy. The brick and concrete walls and floor beaded with condensation. It formed into rivulets that ran down to join, and increase, the puddle from the pipework drip.

The pupils chattered about the show. The girls gathered in the toilets, and amid the slamming of cubicle doors and the splashing of running water from the sink taps they giggled about Penny's costume.

"I wouldn't let people see me like that." said one.

"No way! Gross."

"No one would want to see you anyway." came a catty

response.

"I bet Gemma would want Mr Scarings to see her like that."

"Nah, she wants him to see all of her."

"She wants to see all of him."

"Yuk! That's disgusting."

Adult members of the audience ignored the girls' exchange.

In the gents toilets the boys arrived at a consensus summed up by one as "phwoor!"

Penny sat in her dressing room and drank a cup of tea.

The safety curtain was dropped in, and Tim climbed his ladder and flew in the advertising.

Behind these barriers the crew positioned trucks ready for the start of Act two. Cast, crew and musicians took the opportunity for a quick drink. For once the timpanist stayed in the pit munching a sandwich. He'd chosen to buy chicken from the display of pre-packaged sandwiches in the store on his way into the theatre from his digs. As he started the second diagonally cut round of sliced bread the advertising began to fly out above him. He now knew what was the source of the dust on his drums. He sheltered his food from the stuff coming down. He made an angry mental note to have a word with the orchestra 'fixer' about this. He would speak to him straight after this performance.

"What do you think of the show so far?" Nick shouted back o Miss Robinson over the intervening row of seats using a deliberately jocular phrase.

Miss Robinson was on her feet, worriedly and ineffectually

trying to count the pupils back into their seats. It was a somewhat hopeless task. She could see 'B' and 'C' rows when, for fleeting moments, everyone was seated. Her own row could only be viewed sidelong, and spotting gaps was difficult. She believed the interval to be coming to an end. She didn't know what should be done if, as she feared, some of her charges failed to return.

"We need to count them back in Mr. Arthur."

"Unlike you, I think they're enjoying it. They'll be back."

"But if they're not? We're responsible for them you know."

The pupils between the teachers pulled faces at this. They disliked being treated as children, even if technically they were. Miss Robinson's attitude provoked a rebellious response. In any case, the pupils reasoned, what could possibly happen to them in a theatre.

'She worries too much, that one' thought Norah, helping herself to another of her 'Imperials' and eyeing the worried teacher beside her with some sympathy.

In fact the pupils were all keen to return. The music and spectacle had them riveted and the boys hoped to see more of Penny. In the front of house areas the speakers advised the audience to 'take your seats now please, The performance will continue in five minutes.' As this was said the safety curtain rose to reveal 'The Imperial's lush house tabs again.

Megan gave her 'Act two beginners' calls, and shortly the second half began. Over a thousand customers had been served at the various kiosks, mobile trolleys and bars. The foyers had filled and emptied again. The audience had found its way back to its seats, and the house-lights dimmed exactly on time for a fifteen minute interval. 'The Imperial' delivered this miracle of service and speed twice nightly most days, yet it passed unobserved by the customers. Like any professional operation serving large numbers of customers the theatre relied on expertise developed through years of constant practice among its staff.

With the public areas once more deserted that staff set about restocking shelves, washing glasses and emptying rubbish bins. Paula Morley's aunt, and the rest of the cleaning staff, arrived to begin the routine of between performance cleaning. They were scheduled to commence this with the toilets. They started with a tea break instead.

"Mt niece is watching the show today."

"On her own?"

"No. She's with a school party."

"Oh god! School parties. 'Ow many of them 'ave they got in?" said one.

"Too many." the supervisor declared. "Dirty little tykes. There'll be litter all over the floor when we get in there," she nodded head towards the auditorium, "and the loos'll be a bloody mess."

In the cramped cleaners' cupboard, where they were perched on upturned buckets and boxes of cleaning supplies they could hear the show's music as a faint, but persistent rhythmic thump, punctuated occasionally by the sound of applause. Paula's aunt shifted her overweight form uncomfortably and sipped her tea.

The second act's first major set piece was the seven deadly sins sequence. Dr. Faustus and Helen of Troy stood to one side of the stage on a small rostrum watching the chorus singing and dancing their way though the number. It was actually seven numbers, segued together as a continuous piece of music, with the dancers rotated from section to section to allow for costume changes.

Penny was more discreetly dressed for this act, if a flimsy gold Greek style smock dress cut so low in the neckline that her breasts were near to falling out, and so short that the stalls could see her gold sequinned knickers could be called 'discreet'.

The lack of exposure on the part of the leading lady was more than compensated for for the members of the audience for whom this was an important factor, such as the boys in the school parties, by the dancers' costumes. Some of the girls that Patsy considered 'slutty' nudged each other and giggled at bulges in tighter male dancer costumes. Whatever 'sin' was being featured the designers had produced a visual spectacle worthy of the most outrageous imagination of Hieronymus Bosch.

While Megan played on, with her queen in deeper and deeper trouble, the cast performed the routines for Gluttony, Greed, Sloth, Wrath, Envy, Pride and eventually Lust,

Megan was finding herself falling victim to 'wrath' as a series of stupid errors on her part with her chess game were taken advantage of by her follow-spot operator opponent. She was annoyed with herself for these mistakes, and slightly angry that the young follow-spot operator was besting her on this occasion.

At the railway station an incredibly long delayed train had pulled in. Among the jaded and cross passengers who burst from its opening doors was Tom. He stepped onto a platform along which his fellow travellers were hurrying. He looked at his watch. Now he would need to kill time until he could speak to Megan. He made his way to the main exit from the Victorian station, through a small forest of ornate wrought iron supports, and down a short wide flight of steps which had originally formed an imposing entrance, but now were topped by a confused mess of modern plastic signs with the sides of the flight obstructed by concrete ramps.

He came out into a clammy drizzle. Pausing for a while in front of a back-lit map of the city he managed to orientate himself and set off for a long tramp through the rain along South Parade. He was going in the opposite direction to most of the crowds on the pavements, as the homeward trek of workers was still largely intent on getting to the station he'd just left. By the time he reached a point on the road facing 'The Imperial' he was tired of dodging the advancing pedestrians, none of whom seemed willing to alter their path to accommodate oncoming people, and went for shelter in a brassy tea and coffee bar from where he could see the theatre if he wiped the window and peered to the left. He perched on an over-high stool against the red plastic shelf warming his hands around yet another cardboard cup of tea and settled down to wait.

Dan was fed up with Simon, and Simon was fed up with being trapped in the truck. In the child's mind the thrill of driving in the big vehicle with his dad had waned as the day had worn on and boredom had set in. He'd asked is father repeatedly when they would be finished, and the promises of 'just a few more' deliveries no longer pacified him. His view of the world was no longer exciting. He'd only really been able to see anything of interest out of the side windows, as he wasn't tall enough to see much more than the roofs of any other vehicle they were following and the upper floors of the passing buildings through the cleared part of the windscreen swept by the wipers. The rain had covered his side window long ago, and had gone through big blobs, big blobs that ran down and into each other to produce rivulets which sometimes went side ways if the lorry was going fast enough, to the present wet effect which was an almost opaque frosting, caused by the fine mist type of rain that the city was under at present.

He started to whine.

Dan initially tried to jolly him along. He pointed out sights that might interest a small boy. But naturally many of these were invisible to the child and Simon was not to be mollified. Dan tried the bribery of sweets, but even that inducement palls after a while.

Now Dan was getting cross. He was just one drop from completing his round for the day. He'd saved this drop till last though he knew it would be a long task. He delivered regularly to this firm. Their premises were in a yard off a narrow lane almost exactly facing Wellington Street. The lane was far too narrow for any vehicle. The major drawback with this company was, however, that their security systems were such that any delivery had to be allowed into the yard, and then given admittance to the appropriate building in the yard. If the delivery included items for more than one department within the company the whole security process had to be undergone for each building.

This was going to mean leaving Simon in the cab for some time. Dan drove down the length of South Parade in the heavy traffic, past the theatre and turned left into Wellington Street. As he had hoped there was nothing parked there and he was able to pull in with his nearside wheels just on the pavement alongside the blank brick wall near the corner. Ahead of where he stopped a lamp-post guarded the edge of one of the exit doors with its large lettering instructing 'Keep Clear'. The wide pavement here left ample room for any pedestrians, and he could unload while still allowing any traffic to pass him. He had done this many times before.

"Last delivery, Simon." he told his son, "It might take quite a while, but you'll have to stop here. You'll be all right won't you? And when I get back we'll go home."

"OK Dad." his son replied with a sigh.

Dan put the lorry in neutral, made sure the handbrake was on, turned off the engine and climbed down from the cab. He went to the back and released the catches on the tail-gate lift and dropped the platform down to its horizontal position. Climbing into the back he moved the last remaining pallet of boxes onto the pallet truck and ran it onto the tail-gate. The lift went down when he pressed the button, and he pulled the load off it onto the road. The boxes swayed a bit unsteadily as the truck's small wheels transferred from the flat bed of the lift to the cambered tarmac surface of the road. He pressed the button and sent the lift back up and secured it.

Dan walked back around to the cab and opened the driver's door a bit.

"Daddy's going now. I'll be as quick as I can."

He got a sad bored look as a reply and felt guilty as he shut the driver's door before heading off to deliver his boxes. He saw, as he went, that with this load he was unlucky enough to be having to deliver to three different departments. He hoped that someone at the firm might take pity on him, but he doubted it. The boxes started to change to a darker colour on their exposed faces as the rain wetted them as he waited to cross South Parade.

Chapter 16

The plenum ventilation and heating system vacillated the louvres on its intake and extract in response to the heat rising from the packed house and the clammy chill air that it sometimes sucked in from the rain drenched roof above the theatre's front of house. Technically a hysteresis loop was in operation here, where the response time of various thermostats and the mechanical delays of the motors operating the louvres meant that the system's flow could not change from bringing air in to blowing hot air out too rapidly or frequently. The original design had worked well for many decades. Successive repairs and replacements had upset the balance of the system gradually, though no-one had been aware, so that though the auditorium temperature was still held at the desired level this was now done by far too many and too frequent changes of the louvres.

Inside the auditorium Charlie thought that the seven deadly sins sequence was one of the best continuous pieces of musical theatre he had seen. Clearly the audience agreed with him. To his left he could see the public was mesmerised by the performance. The reflected glow of the stage lighting let him observe that the usual occasional movement of hands to sweet bags and then to mouths was stilled as the punters absorbed this piece. Even the school parties seemed to be concentrating. The family in the neighbouring box that he had looked at earlier seemed to be spellbound.

The sequence drew towards its 'lust' end, with Brian and Penny leaving their position almost below him to cross slowly to the opposite side of the stage, followed obediently by some of the moving heads so that they were prominently featured against a writhing background of dancers. Penny's brief costume was rendered semi transparent by the backlight.

"F6 to H5" said the lime operator's voice in Megan's

headphones.

She was not doing well on this occasion. The show's challenging scene change was fast approaching. She really didn't ought to be worrying about losing a queen. As the seven deadly sins came to a close, to thunderous applause, she made a hasty decision and said:

"E5 to F7"

She followed this with a mass of standby calls. On stage a few lines of dialogue were taking place. The scene change started in full view and the orchestra underscore hinted at the next number, the hit 'Devil May Care'.

Sandy James suddenly felt a fierce recurrence of his heartburn. He ploughed on through his blocked moves, but the pain was overwhelming. His vision seemed to go out of focus. He felt dizzy. His disorientation was increased by the scenic trucks now moving to their new positions. The one he should be next to swung past him towards the prompt-side wing. As it reached its position he stretched out a hand to steady himself. The slight additional push forced the truck off its mark and the spring loaded pin that had caused trouble earlier in the run at The Imperial once again failed to seat properly. On this occasion the crew did not notice. Frank was readying himself in the wings next to Megan.

"H5 to F4, takes your queen." said the voice in her ear.

"Sod it!"

The cues continued to be given without interruption. In response the trucks swung outwards on their pivots. The prompt side truck moved off its centre. Part of the steel framed scenic content passed outside the proscenium arch. Like an out-flung arm the higher part smashed into the trussing bearing moving head number twenty three.

At precisely that moment head number twenty three was turning to a new position. It had been plotted do do this at speed, as cues were thick and fast.

Charlie flinched back on his balcony as the impact occurred just inches from him. He was, perhaps the first person to realise that something had gone wrong. The family in the adjacent box must have realised too, a moment later, as he heard, above the music, a distinct startled scream.

Unaware, with her eyes on monitors that didn't show the collision, Megan started the cues for Frank's entrance.

Simon's boredom was at a peak. He pushed his toy lorry back and forth with ever greater aggression. Then, suddenly, the toy slipped from his hand and fell to the cab floor. For a few moments he struggled in vain to reach it. Frustrated he sulked. Then with guilty hands, for he knew that he wasn't allowed to, he fumbled with the buckle on his seat belt, pressing the square red button until it came undone. He climbed off the seat and down into the foot-well to retrieve the toy. He could stand up quite easily in the space and saw that he could climb over into the driver's seat. The temptation was too great. In seconds he was sat in his father's place.

The slight fear of discovery gave way to the excitement of 'driving' the lorry. He sat on the edge of the driver's position and made 'brummm brummm' noises as he clutched the steering wheel in childish hands.

He found he could swing the wheel left and right a little bit. He became absorbed in his own fantasy world of driving the big vehicle along imaginary roads. Sometimes he made engine noises, sometimes he tried to simulate the sound of tyre squeal. His wrenching of the steering grew more violent. He had totally forgotten how he had been frequently told not to touch. His little hand reached out and wiggled the gear lever. Back to the steering wheel. Left. Right Left..... There was a strange click, and the wheel would not move any more.

The boy didn't understand why. He didn't know about steering locks, and the one on the truck had now engaged, with the wheels turned slightly left.

Frightened, he made desperate efforts to remedy whatever it was he had done. At random he tried all the odd levers that stuck out from the steering column. Had the ignition been on indicators would have flashed, wipers would have wiped, windscreen washers would have washed. Simon's efforts had no effect at all.

The child began an ever broader and illogical search.

Wiggling the gear stick did nothing. This was the handbrake wasn't it? It went 'hiss' when Daddy used it. Perhaps it had to be the other way to free the steering wheel. He pulled and pushed. The lever failed to move. He suddenly remembered, he'd seen Daddy pull up on the yellow ring below the knob. He tried, but his small hand was not strong enough.

Simon was frantic now. He was starting to cry. In panic he became convinced that he must free the steering wheel that his childish mind told him he had broken. He slid off the seat and stood on the floor facing back towards the brake. Grasping the yellow lock ring with both hands he pushed and pulled. Without warning the ring moved upwards and the lever snapped backwards. He turned and reached up to the wheel. Still it would not move. But something was happening. From his place on the cab floor he could see straight up through the rain spattered windscreen and the tops of the buildings were moving. Very slowly, but they were moving.

With the brake released Dan's lorry began to roll down the slope of Wellington Street. The steering lock held its track slightly to the left. The nearside wheels were already on the path. By the time the off side reached the curb the truck had gathered enough momentum for these wheels to mount the path. Simon felt the slight bump as the offside wheels bounced onto the pavement but still didn't understand what was happening. Now there was a smooth surface beneath the vehicle. It gathered pace angling gently towards the side of The Imperial. The front of the van just passed inside the lamp-post which the end of the bumper missed by less than an inch. Within a second the near side met the brickwork. The lorry slid another few feet along the wall making a scraping noise that terrified the child. The hollow interior of the empty rear body magnified the noise, and the ripping of the near side wing by the bricks was a long drawn out grinding from which even young Simon could imagine terrible damage. Eventually it came to a halt, tightly jammed between the post and the theatre. The side panels of the box were exactly across the exit from the upper circle.

Simon's terror at what he had done caused him to burst into hysterical crying. He huddled down below the steering wheel in the foot well near the pedals. He cried for his mummy, with such passion that his tears were soon making him gasp for breath between sobs.

Charlie backed away from his balcony rail. There was barely a moment's hesitation before he turned and ran through his office behind him, and out into the front of house corridor on the upper circle level. His ornately panelled dark mahogany door, bearing the single gold lettered word 'private', slammed behind him as he sprinted for the stairs. Two doors leading down faced him roughly opposite his office. To the right one set of double doors was conspicuous by its 'Exit' sign. Straight ahead was a single wood panelled door very similar to his office which was lettered, in the same painted gold typeface 'Staff Only'.

He crashed through the single door onto a steep staircase with plain steel handrails either side of the concrete steps. He dropped forward from the top step, grabbing a handrail in each hand about half way down the flight and swinging his feet out and forward to jump onto the first landing. He'd cleared the whole set of stairs in one bound. The landing turned through a hundred and eighty degrees so the next flight doubled back on the first. Charlie bounced off the wall of the landing, turned and repeated his wild leap down the next set of stairs. This brought him to the circle level. Here the staircase became wider, and his handrail grabbing trick was no longer possible. He raced down the zig-zag of the next two flights taking the treads two and three at a time. Once at the stalls level he was in a private passageway that ran from front of house to a pass door to backstage. He was only a few paces from the pass door. 'Stage. No Admittance' said six inch high red block letters across the white panel screwed to the door. Charlie hurled it open, but even now, even under these circumstances, the instinctive engrained training of years of backstage work made him do so as quietly as his haste would allow. He arrived in the downstage prompt corner, a few feet behind Megan. Bare seconds had passed since the truck had collided with the lighting equipment.

Unaware Megan had carried on cueing. Lighting changed, and Frank had leaped onto the stage from the wings. The Devil had come from hell for Faustus' soul. There was a short musical link, no more than a fanfare really, and in those few bars the rig's moving heads panned and tilted, their beams made visible by haze pumped in from both sides.

All except for head number twenty-three. The shock of the impact caused the weakened side of the yoke to deform releasing the tilt bearing on that side, and the notched drive belt ran off the edge of its drive wheel. Under complex centrifugal forces created by the three dimensional motion the main body of the head dropped on one side, hesitated momentarily and pulled clear of the bearing on the other side of the yoke. It might have been possible to calculate the exact expected trajectory of the suddenly freed heavy lamp housing, lenses and all its associated colour and gobo wheels using Newtonian physics. That calculation would have required information on the direction and speed of rotation of the head in both planes at the moment it broke free. As luck would have it the actual flight of the head took a curved path that caused it to smash into the fake pillar of the proscenium arch just a few feet above the stage floor mainly because the split second resistance of the spade connectors on the few bits of wiring between the yoke and the head which made the ill fated light behave as a pendulum in its last moments.

The century old hollow pillar's skin broke under this impact. The head penetrated the ornate painted surface and through the underlying wire mesh former. By chance the point of impact was at a weak place midway between two of the timber frames.

As Megan said 'go' for the pyrotechnics cue that would emphasise Frank's entrance, for all these things were happening at once and no-one could have understood the situation immediately, the operator turned the arming key and pressed the button. A row of flash boxes, each loaded with a plastic cartridge containing an electric detonator and a pile of flash-powder all received a current from the firer and the detonators fired simultaneously. In each flash-pod this detonation ignited the flash powder which went off in a blaze of magnesium white light and a shower of sparks. One of the boxes was on the corner of the stage right next to the proscenium pillar.

What Megan did notice as she gave the 'go' for the pyrotechnics was Sandy, clutching himself with one hand and holding the back of the prompt side truck nearest to her with the other as he slid to the floor.

"Sandy!" she said, urgently, but quietly enough not to be heard by the audience, and she turned upstage towards him.

It was a movement that saved her.

On the fly floor the noise of the truck's collision had been almost as loud as it had been in the boxes adjacent to the proscenium. Tim naturally ran to the fly-rail and was now peering over the edge and down towards the prompt corner in an attempt to see what had happened.

Most of the audience had not so far realised that there was a problem.

Penny's radio mic was still live when, quite involuntarily, she exclaimed

"Oh my God!"

Members of the audience who noticed this as it was amplified over the PA and mixed into the continuing musical score thought it was a reaction to the Devil's entrance.

The timpanist was the first member of the orchestra to register the oncoming disaster. The collision of the truck with the lighting had been more or less straight above his head and he had instinctively looked upward to see where the noise had come from. He was the only real witness to the flight of head number twenty three. The head seemed to him to be coming down on top of him. For a split second he could see straight down the lens towards the cooling lamp, still glowing red as the unit flew through the air. In a panic of self preservation he abandoned his instruments and dived for the illusory cover of the orchestra pit rail. Immediately the head hit the pillar and the air around filled with huge quantities of the dust he had come to hate so much at The Imperial.

The accumulation of years of dusty shavings from the advertising rag's ropes chafing had covered every ledge and crevice inside the fake pillar of the proscenium. When hit by head number twenty-three great clouds of this dust stirred up within the shaft. The outer skin of the pillar was broken by the impact, allowing it to be agitated still more by the inrush of auditorium air.

There is a well known danger from dust particles in grain stores and the like. At certain concentrations a mere spark can ignite the cloud with explosive results. This was not the sort of risk that anyone would have considered for a theatre in their wildest dreams, but today the fates conspired to create the most dangerous conditions possible. A largely enclosed shaft of a pillar, some three feet in diameter and well over twenty feet high had had its dust content stirred into a highly volatile fog. Even so under most conditions nothing would have happened except for a few people in the immediate vicinity choking slightly on the dust. But Megan had cued the firing of the pyrotechnics, and some of the white hot magnesium flash powder content of the flash-pod nearest to the pillar was thrown up into the air and angled itself inside the hole created by the impact of the head.

Instantaneously the dust in the pillar exploded. It exploded with the force of dynamite. The particles lit and burned in a chain reaction of incredible speed, the explosion spreading outwards powerfully.

For the first micro second or two the explosion was channelled upwards by the confining sides of the pillar. The ball of fire burst from the top and went out onto the auditorium ceiling and under the proscenium arch and up on the on-stage side of it.

Tim, on the fly floor, was the first to die. As he leant over the rail the top half of his body caught the full impact of the fireball. His hair and flesh was instantly cremated, and his already lifeless body was flung backwards across the fly-floor to stop, slumped and horribly disfigured against the hauling ropes.

The second or third micro second saw the fake pillar shatter from the expanding gasses inside.

Four members of the audience, unlucky enough to be on that end of A and B rows of the stalls, died then, sliced and cut by flying debris and burned by the expanding fireball. A dozen or so others were badly injured.

Frank was caught in the back by the force of the explosion as he was mid-step in his running entrance. He was hurled clear over the edge of the stage and into the orchestra pit. The orchestra was very lucky. Players on the prompt side of the pit were protected from the worst of the blast by the stage edge, and the timpanist had dived for cover. Frank landed among the violinists, knocking them to the floor and smashing instruments to matchwood. There were some minor injuries, but the Devil saved the players from more serious harm.

The explosion itself caused two further serious bits of damage to the fabric of The Imperial. Immediately below the stage floor the power and control cables for the entire lighting system were torn apart.

Adrian found himself suddenly confronted by a blank monitor screen and a control desk which changed from a mass of red, green and yellow LED indicators to a black dead panel in a dark auditorium. All the stage lighting snapped to blackout except for the back bar of movers which, due to their setting, began to wave randomly across the front of the stage and the auditorium for a few seconds while the units searched for a control signal that would not come again, before pointing straight up towards the grid.

Deep in the cellars the concussion of the explosion broke the tenuous hold that the new pipework join had. The pipes parted, and the boiling output began to fountain around the room, hissing as it splashed hot surfaces on the boilers themselves. Far up in the roof the hot radiators in the plenum inlet suddenly cooled. The boiling water rapidly flooded the boiler house and the steam and liquid forced its way into the adjacent electrical areas shorting out whole sections of the installation.

Tom had been studying the front of The Imperial through the café window. At ground floor level the entrance was glowing out into the dusk, with the lights shining off the highly polished brass handles of the doors. Either side the lit poster boards proudly announced "Faustus!". Further up the building the brickwork was interspersed with carved stonework. Centrally above the doors the architect had placed the traditional comedy and tragedy masks, but here positioned between, and apparently supported by, a throng of cherubs, all now smeared in shades of darker grey and green by the weather of ten decades. Small round or gothic windows scattered the frontage, but like most theatres the builder's objective was to keep daylight out. At the top of the building mock battlements hid most of the rooftop mechanics. Tom could see a wisp of steam rising. He rightly guessed it was from the heating and ventilation system. Absently he watched it rising and vanishing in the drizzle.

Inside Charlie, arriving in the moment immediately after the explosion, leaped forward and grabbed the release for the safety curtain. He beat Ben to it by the merest margin. A small soft toy devil, knocked from the stage management desk by the force of the blast, got under their feet and was kicked to lie against the wall. Chess pieces rolled. The iron began to descend across the proscenium. Neither Charlie nor Ben had ever expected to use it in a real situation. In fact Charlie was still mentally preparing himself for being told that he had overreacted. The thought was stopped as the iron hit the top of the steel framed piece of scenery that had started the problem with the collision with the lighting truss. The heavy fire curtain paused, stationary. Then after an agonising couple of seconds there was a grinding and creaking as the scenery buckled out of shape to allow the safety curtain to fall.

Brian and Penny had been facing the disaster. They were lucky to be far enough away to escape hurt, though they were knocked over backwards. Brian scrambled to his feet, seized Penny's hand and dragged her upstage in the momentary delay as the iron descended behind them sealing them safely away from the auditorium.

The descent of the iron also sealed the auditorium from the last vestiges of light coming from the upstage moving heads. The house was lit only by the dim glimmer of the scattered emergency lights and the flickering of the flames. There was a brief pause in which the audience's bewildered minds refused to accept what they had just seen. Some at first believed it to be a hugely spectacular special effect and part of the show. Their realisation was slow.

All over the venue people were confused, or failing to have registered the catastrophe. Megan's whole attention had been on Sandy at the moment of the crisis, and she had stepped forward and dropped to her knees beside him as he fell. At once the enormity of the accident dawned on her.

"House-lights, house-lights!" she shouted into her headset microphone.

"I bloody can't!" answered Alistair, "There's no bloody power."

The stage was suddenly flooded with bland white light as Charlie found the working lights switches. Megan became aware of how quiet it had become. The music had stopped mid bar and it was as if everyone was holding their breath.

Jane had been crossing the stage moving some props into position. Now she ran to Sandy's side. The working lights revealed him grey and limp.

"Help me someone." Jane begged.

Susie had heard the explosion, and sudden cessation of the show over the show relay speakers in the dressing rooms and had run to the stage to see what was happening. She came through the door into the prompt side wing just in time to hear Jane. Seeing Sandy, for whom she had been so concerned, she guessed that he had had a heart attack. She pulled her mobile phone from her pocket and rang 999 to ask for an ambulance. It was the first of many 999 calls that would be made in the next few minutes.

Chapter 17

As Tom watched there was a brief gout of dense black smoke from the top of The Imperial where there had previously been gentle steam. He was startled by this. It lasted very few seconds but it was solid and menacing. It looked much more than a simple venting of boiler-house smoke. He looked about to see if anyone else had noticed, but they were talking, texting or just staring at their coffees.

The fire had spread speedily to run across, above and below the ceiling, burning timbers and cables. It was the cables that produced the thick choking smoke that roiled over the auditorium. Some of it was sucked into the extract shafts of the ventilation and up to the rooftop extract louvres. The house was hot, the flaps were open to allow old hot air out and fresh air in. The system pumped a cloud of the filthy smoke out. As it did so the temperature in the inlet radiators, which had managed to stay up to the required level despite the interval demand on hot water, dropped suddenly and dramatically because of the hot water draining from the system through the fracture in the pipe in the cellar. The louvres shut, cutting off the tell tale escape of smoke from the roof and trapping the choking fumes inside.

In the auditorium the moment of stunned silence had ended. A single sprinkler jet began discharging water onto the devastated corner of A and B row with a penetrating hiss. It drenched the survivors, but mainly missed the seat of the flames. The darkness was lifted slightly by the dozens of mobile phones which the audience switched on, either as torches or to video and photograph the incident. The light from these waved wildly and mostly uselessly.

And the screaming started.

It took some time for the front of house staff to become aware of the situation. Insulated from the auditorium noise, and not inside watching the audience, usherettes and management lost minutes before rushing to their pre-planned positions for evacuation. The house manager entered the rear of the stalls, trying in vain to shout his message of 'no cause for alarm' and 'please leave quietly by the exits'. He could not be heard. He was pushed aside by the first members of the public fighting to get out of the doors.

At most exits ushers or usherettes opened the curtains and doors entreating 'this way out please'.

Someone, somewhere broke the glass in a fire alarm point, and the growing panic and confusion was made worse by the unnecessary screaming sirens that were triggered by this.

John Mason woke groggily in the house manager;s office and pulled himself upright to go out into the foyer. The swarming crowd swept him out into the street where two police cars were passing in the slow traffic, nose to tail, heading back to their station from a shift. John reeled against the bonnet of the first one. The convoy halted, and John would have been in for at least a telling off, for his slightly slurred explanations were forcefully thrust aside by the policemen, but for the cries of 'fire' that the officers became aware of when they finally actually got out of their cars. Reacting unusually quickly they logged their fastest ever response time and also gave impetus to the calls to the fire brigade that were starting to be received by the services.

Their contribution to the crisis was more arguable. Unsure what to do they proceeded to set up barricades around the front of the theatre and across the South Parade end of Wellington Street. These were intended to hold back any crowds, but initially only corralled the evacuating audience in a tight area around the burning Imperial. Aside from hurrying audience members there was little outward sign of the fire. Tom had seen the only burst of smoke that had so far escaped. No injured had yet emerged, and a casual look would have shown no more than what appeared to be a normal end of show exodus.

The House Manager was in the stalls demanding, in the gloom, that the sound engineer give him a microphone. There were no microphones normally in use at the mixer position, and the engineer was rummaging around in boxes and flight cases under the desk to find one to plug in for him. They were buffeted by passing public while he hunted. When he finally did get a mic into the House Manager's hand only one side of the PA system turned out to be working due to damage to the cables caused by the explosion. Power for the out-front mixer had been laid in from the rear of the auditorium, and had stayed on. The amplifier racks on stage had equally miraculously continued to work.

"There is no cause for alarm..." sounded very unconvincing.

The house manager attempted a calming tone of voice, but against a background of shouts and screams and amplified to be heard above these it smacked of plaintive wheedling broadcast lop-sidedly across the crowd.

"... no cause for alarm. The situation is under control. May we ask you to make your way quietly..."

He could ask all he liked. In the stalls a mass of pushing and shoving public was intent on the doors. In the front rows a few, a very few, were attempting to administer some sort of comfort and first aid to those who had been hurt. No-one had any equipment, or knew where to find it, and handkerchiefs and torn shirts were being pressed against wounds. The theatre's own first-aid staff were unable to reach the front of the stalls because of the press of bodies coming out.

Tom was concerned. The smoke had made him tense and sit up on his stool. The arrival of the police convinced him that something had happened. He abandoned his tea and came out into the street and crossed to the barrier that was being erected, joining a growing crowd of the curious on one side trying to get in, as the audience tried to get out. People were shouting, demanding information. He gleaned fragments of news. There had been an explosion, There had been a fire. The completely unfounded conclusion was being spread abroad by panic mongers of a terrorist attack. There was no justification for this, no reason for anyone to make the assumption, but once said the rumour caused a toughening of the police's already erroneous handling of the incident. The wailing of distant sirens preceded the arrival of yet more police, starting with two motor-cycle cops. They set about bullying the crowd, trying to move them on. Fortunately the nearest terrorist response unit was some thirty miles away so the victims were spared that additional intervention.

Tom held his ground.

"Move aside, keep moving."

"My girlfriend's in there."

Was she his girlfriend? Had she ever really been? Did he want her to be? He'd made this long unpleasant journey to get her to return, but largely to pay the bills. Was he in love? Had the two of them ever been in love? Certainly they'd shared some lust, and he still felt lust for her curvy body, but 'love'? It was a dilemma he'd debated with himself countless times now since their split. Sometimes he could convince himself that the very fact of the internal debate showed that he cared about her. At other times he admitted the purely financial attraction of having his accommodation and bills secured by her regular income. Sometimes, mostly in his solo bed at night, he indulged in fantasies. Just now he was certain he wanted to get into the theatre and see what had happened to Megan. The police had other ideas, and shoved him and other bystanders away.

He started trying to dodge round the temporary barriers and their guards, but it was the audience pouring out that really prevented him getting in. The audience wanted to leave, they were on mobile phones ringing and texting friends and trapped in the enclosure.

Next to him at the barrier a large middle aged woman was taking 'selfie' pictures. He could imagine the social media captions that would be there in the next few seconds. 'Me at the incident at The Imperial', 'Me in the crowd' and, he thought, it was likely once the inevitable arrival of the anti terror squad happened 'Me being shoved out of the way'.

"This is really neat," she said to him, "I was just passing, and now I'm going to be on the news, once the TV people get here."

"I'm trying to get to my girlfriend."

"Where is she then?" she asked absently.

"She's in the theatre, she's stage managing the show."

His reply produced a burst of interest from her. She shuffled about in the crowd so she was standing side by side with him, held her phone out in front of them and took a picture. 'Me with someone who knows someone in the theatre' he thought.

"We had an argument."

"Yeah." He detected an accent now. Probably American he decided.

"So I've come to get her back. And I need to know that she's all right. I need her back. I need her back to pay the bills..." He tailed off, aware that he'd finally voiced the true situation, and a bit ashamed to have let a complete stranger hear him.

She was not listening, her attention was now on the distant end of South Parade over her left shoulder where more approaching sirens could be heard as the fire brigade slowly struggled through the now log jammed traffic.

Susie and Jane had been joined by a couple of members of the chorus. Enthusiastic, if inexpert, cardiac massage was being performed on Sandy.

Charlie and Ben were both wielding extinguishers, trying to put out the minor fires that were scattered around the prompt corner on the stage side of the barrier of the safety curtain. Flames could be seen running along the timber of the fly-rail above them.

"Where the hell is Tim?" Charlie demanded, "Ben, get up there and sort that before it gets a hold or burns through a rope."

"OK. Will you get the cast and the rest of the crew out?"

Ben made for the fly-floor. He looked back to check on Megan. He found it was suddenly very important to him that she should be safely out of the theatre.

Megan was back in command and paging the dressing rooms and starting to order the cast off the stage out of the building. None of the cast, or the touring crew, had any idea where the assembly points were. Notices had been completely ignored on arrival. But they knew where the stage door was, and were making that way. It made no difference where they gathered outside, those who'd been on stage when the explosion occurred were making for the street with haste. Brian pushed Penny ahead of him through the cast filled passages and out into the open air. They couldn't see much that was happening on South Parade when they looked up the street towards it, as a large van was stopped right against the wall of the theatre. To see further they had to sprawl out into the roadway. And they did. Soon the area around the stage door was thronged with musicians, mostly clutching instruments, some of which were broken, crew, and cast in startlingly revealing costumes. Members of the public held away from the front of the theatre, or leaving the stalls to discover themselves trapped by the police barriers, turned down the hill of Wellington Street and found they were mingling with the thespians, musicians and staff.

Wet and bedraggled though they quickly became the cast were the object of great interest to the public. Phone cameras were out here too, especially once the stars were spotted. Penny's costume became transparent in the rain and the images of her wet, revealed and shivering went viral almost immediately.

Susie eventually arrived with a dressing gown for Penny, leaving Sandy to others, but the bulk of the cast huddled miserably in their skimpy clothes. For those who'd been near the explosion and fire now shock began to set in, and this combined with the wet to make many of them start to shake uncontrollably.

"Where's Frank? Penny asked plaintively. The experience of being photographed in this revealing garb looking less than her best was, she had discovered, quite different from deliberate posed erotic exposure. For the first time she doubted her decisions to show off her body.

"I don't know. I expect he's all right. Why?" Susie had not seen the moment of the explosion.

"He got blown off the stage. He fell in the pit."

"Oh God! I didn't know. I'll go and find out." and she was off through the throng of actors hunting for him.

She found him in the midst of a group of musicians who'd

made their way up from the orchestra pit. The musicians were in foul moods due to the damaged instruments, many trying to get Susie's attention to voice their complaints. Susie's concern was for Frank. Bruised and battered he made a sorry looking and bedraggled Devil. The back of his costume was scorched from the explosion and he had cuts on his face and hands from the sharp bits of instruments and music stands that he had landed on.

Susie set about trying to get some first aid assistance for him. It was a thankless task in the confused shambles that existed outside the stage door. She wished now that she had learnt first aid, but like most she had never expected to be in a situation like this.

Chapter 18

The smoke rolled towards the Upper Circle first. The emergency lighting was made dimmer as it drifted in front of the fittings. Most of the public in the two circles had been dazzled by the random sweepings of the upstage moving lights before the iron's descent cut off the beams. John Scarings scrambled out of his seat and turned toward the exit through which they had entered, several rows up the slope of the floor from where he was, and already showing a dull foggy blur above it where the green exit light was obscured by the smoke.

Patsy Newbon also leaped to her feet, closely followed by Gemma. Patsy faced down the slope. She and John confronted each other just one row apart in the gloom. She was terrified, but her understanding of the science behind their situation made her display a very rare flash of determination.

"Down!" she shouted above the growing din. "Down! Below the smoke." and she pointed over John's shoulder at the doorway leading to the stairs down to street level.

Gemma saw John's face fleetingly in the light of a wavering phone. Correctly she read concern, tenderness and, yes maybe love in his expression. Her teenage emotions burst forward again, though during the show she'd gone through annoyance at the thwarting of her designs in the seating, a seething hatred for his callous treatment of her desire and then reluctantly being absorbed in the show. Now her crush rushed back. He was worried for her, He had turned to see that she was all right in this frightening situation. John would get her away from here, and his concern for her welfare meant that he had realised that he cared for her. They would be together, his rescue of her from this terror would seal their relationship. He would.....

And the torch beam of an unsteady phone swept back across John, and Gemma's briefly resurrected hopes were dashed when she saw where exactly he was looking, and realised who the emotions she had read into his face were for. Miss Newbon. John turned away and Patsy grabbed Gemma's shoulder saying "Come on!".

Behind Gemma other pupils were starting to push along the row. she started to move out of the seating. Patsy set off down the slope toward the exit, encouraging the pupils in 'C' row to move on too. Gemma's eyes filled with tears not only because of the smoke. She had her hand on the arm of Patsy's seat next to the gangway. A shove from behind her caused her to overbalance as the arm came partly free of the end plate, the sharp edged screw, that Patsy had found, pulling through the worn casting so the arm swung outwards into the gangway on its one remaining fixing.

Gemma fell to the floor just outside the row and in the gangway. Her classmates panicking and rushing stumbled over her. One trod on her outstretched arm and she screamed with pain as the bone snapped. Anonymous feet kicked her in the ribs, the legs, the face, and trampled on her and passed over her to escape. Heavy feet nipped flesh between their soles and the floor painfully. Her cheek was on the carpet and even in her discomfort she was dimly aware of its gritty texture. She could see nothing. The faint emergency lights lost in the smoke failed to penetrate the press of bodies stumbling over her bruised and prone form. Neither Patsy nor John had seen her fall.

John had turned to the exit seizing a dithering Paula Morley and propelling the girl before him to the escape. The exit door from the auditorium gave onto concrete stairs. Urging Paula into a headlong run John began leading the crocodile of pupils down to the ground floor. The stairs were narrow and the pupils could only go down about two abreast. The back and forth turns in the staircase were frequent and close together, so that the staircase took up little floor area within the building.

As John was going down Ben was making his way up another staircase backstage. He passed a few cast members emerging from dressing room corridors at different levels and heading downward in obedience to the tannoyed evacuation call that Megan was now putting out. The call was using the old fashioned traditional code word "Mr Sands" to pass on the information of a fire. However most of the cast had been on stage for the 'deadly sins' so there were only stragglers, lucky enough to be wrapping themselves in coats, over their costumes before venturing into the city street.

Near the top of the staircases Ben saw a figure ahead. Above him, and coming down was the casual who worked with Tim on the fly-floor during performances.

"Hey! What's happening up there?" Ben demanded.

They paused for a moment. The young casual worker stood on the top step of the flight with one leg poised in mid air about to step down. Ben waited at the bottom. The youngster froze, wide eyed, and then, without a word, plunged headlong down the stairs past him and out of sight deeper into the building.

Puzzling and surprised Ben went on up, beyond the upper dressing rooms to the door that led to the fly-floor, seeking Tim. He found his remains against the counterweight hauling ropes, and was immediately violently and involuntarily sick. There was no doubt Tim was dead, though there was some doubt as to his identity, but Ben was sure from where he found the corpse.

A few of the ropes near the proscenium were smouldering, and Ben put these out easily with a fire extinguisher. That done he steeled himself to go back past the grisly thing he had found. He tried edging past, facing away, towards the space above the stage, but awful fascination drew his eyes back as he did so. There was nothing on the fly floor with which to cover the body, so he left as quickly as he could. He came back down the stairs faster than he had gone up.

Patsy stayed on the upper circle, near the exit, with pupils shoving past and around her until she was sure that Nick Arthur and Miss Robinson had risen and were herding the tail end of the school party. It was difficult to be certain, but she could see movement through the smoke if she bent down a little to get below the worst of the cloud. All around pupils, and the audience in general were coughing and choking. She joined the movement to the stairs. General public in 'A' row were also pushing the same way. The young children who'd been on that row were knocked and buffeted by the adults and the teenage pupils. There were many screams and one of the little children, entering the stairwell, began shouting "Mummy, mummy!" in fear.

Its plaintive cries seemed to hit a high frequency that resonated on the hard walls of the stairwell. The child's parents' efforts to reassure it from where they were a few stairs behind were unsuccessful and the cries persisted as the child, it was the boy, was swept on downwards by the tide of people.

Patsy found the stairs almost as dark as the upper circle itself had been, though the smoke had not found its way into the stairwell. She had been right to insist on their taking the downward route out she decided. The construction of the stairs was such that people on one short flight of stairs could not see others on either the section above or below them. The stairs turned around a solid central wall that blocked all view or communication. The flights were tightly packed and short resulting in rather low headroom. Even Patsy could easily reach up and touch the bare flat angled ceiling, which was the underside of the stairs over her head, above her at any point. Crowded with anxious people these stairs were becoming more and more claustrophobic as she made her way down them.

There were strangers either side of her, but she could recognise many of the Thomas Lincoln pupils in front of her in the semi darkness, partly because of their uniforms. She was surprised to find the small child from 'A' row, separated from its parents was squeezed in beside her on her step along with two of her pupils. Really the steps could only fit a couple of adults side by side, but the press from above was making the audience squash tightly into the space. The little boy continued to scream, but Patsy could not bend down to comfort him in the crowded space.

Progress down the stairs was becoming very slow, and she wondered what bottleneck was causing the hold up.

Above; sixteen or seventeen of Gemma's classmates had, mostly unwittingly, stumbled over her battered form. Some realised that someone was on the ground, but the crush made identification or an attempt to assist impossible even had their own fear allowed them to consider it. Row D had been largely boys, and the pushing was more brutal than in other places in the audience.

It was not until Miss Robinson reached the end of the row that Gemma was really noticed. Miss Robinson was frightened too, but not perhaps so much for for her own physical welfare. She was frightened that this ill advised theatre trip might turn out to end in tragedy. Her impeccable, if unexceptional career could not be allowed to be sullied, right at its end, by any harm coming to pupils in her care. That this might be because of a trip to a show that had repulsed her throughout, she ignored the brief parts that she had approved of, added insult to the situation. She determined that she would ensure the pupils' safety. She was less pressed upon by the crowd than many. In fact the only person following her along the row was Norah.

The audience had behaved exactly normally in these abnormal circumstances. Having been directed to their seats via routes that meant that about half of each row had come in from each side they would leave in the direction from which they had come. Human nature meant that this was almost always the case with a group of any sort. People had even been known to make their way into obviously dangerous areas, because that was the way they had come, in incidents of this sort.

Norah had been in two minds which way to go. Her central seat was equidistant from both gangways, and the public to her left did seem to be moving out slightly faster than the school party to her right. But the instinct to retrace her original path won, and she followed Miss Robinson's back, edging slightly sideways between the tipped up seats and the backs of the row in front. She was worried by the column of flame near the stage. Her eyes stung from the smoke, and she was choking in the noxious fumes.

Miss Robinson reached the end of the row, and like all before her trod on Gemma as she emerged onto the gangway. Her sensible shoes had sharp edged chunky heels and one of these dug into Gemma's flesh. She however would not walk over the girl to ensure her escape. It became a major and imperative duty to her to save this pupil, who she vaguely recognised despite the darkness. Stepping back, and colliding with Norah, she bent down and seized the girl's wrist. Hauling on Gemma's broken arm she lifted her to her feet by brute force with a strength she hadn't known she had.

Gemma screamed. A continuous scream punctuated by momentary gasps for breath. In her anguish she hurt in so many places besides her arm that she did not consciously notice the stabbing pain at her hip of the sharp screw head on the arm of the seat jabbing through her skirt and into her flesh. Weak at rhe knees she dangled in Miss Robinson's grasp, impaled on the screw.

"Pull yourself together girl!" Miss Robinson would stand no nonsense from someone she was determined to rescue.
"Stop this silly screaming!"

Gemma's screaming was unabated.

Miss Robinson redoubled her effort and pulled harder on her injured arm. The pain of broken bone grinding caused the girl to draw shuddering breaths. The screw head tore a jagged line of blood down her thigh to her knee, ripping her skirt apart so it fell around her ankles tripping her so her teacher's grasp of her arm took even more weight as she lurched forward. Miss Robinson trod on the material of her uniform on the floor and the girl's feet tangled in it as the two of them stumbled into the crowd.

Moments later Norah too tripped on the discarded skirt as the material snagged on her high heels..

She staggered forward, but was caught and held by a man coming down the gangway from her right.

"Oh, thank you." said gasped.

The man may not have heard in the cacophony around them. A few feet ahead Gemma still shrilly rent the air with her pain. Sporadic cries and shouting came from all sides. The crush was thinning slightly, but an air of confusion and fear was palpable.
Frightened Norah was grateful to lean on the man's arm while she disentangled her feet from the skirt. His wife was clinging to his other arm, then the three of them groped their way towards the stairwell.

Descent down the staircase had stopped. The school-children, teachers and the public who had mingled in with them stood on the steps, squashed and uncomfortable, moving down only the occasional half step as someone changed position. Norah, and her new companions, joined the top end of this log-jammed queue somewhere after the topmost landing turning. Others crammed in behind them. There was an uneasy shifting of weight from one foot to the other by the trapped audience. A few steps below Norah, and separated from her by strangers, and a few pupils from 'Tigger's' row, Gemma had subsided into pained moaning. By lifting her arm with her uninjured hand and hooking fingers into the front of her blouse she had taken the worst of the discomfort from the break. She still suffered whenever a neighbour jostled her but could try to investigate her other hurts. She felt her cheek with her undamaged left hand, it was sore and swelling from a kick during her time on the ground. Lower her ribs ached where feet had walked on her. She felt down to her hip, where sticky blood was running from the gash caused by the screw head in the seat arm. For the first time she realised that she was virtually naked from the waist down. Her skirt was gone, and the screw had ripped her knickers at the side from waistband down, so they hung like rag on the side where she had been injured, held on by just the elastic. Instinctively she tried to gather the front and back together without success. Embarrassed she clamped her thighs tightly as she balanced on her step and tried to pull her blouse further down, though the crowd meant that no-one could see. The bottom of her blouse came low enough to just hide her ragged panties. She flushed red. But all the people on the way to this exit were hot and flushed now, as the air on the stairs grew hotter and more foetid.

Nick Arthur herded the last of the Thomas Lincoln pupils into the stairs, coughing, now the smoke was hanging lower and thicker, but trying indomitably to keep up his usual bonhomie for the youngsters' benefit. Many of them, particularly the girls from his row of seats, were clearly upset and almost hysterical. It was mainly due to Nick's skills that real panic was averted on that side of the Upper Circle.

By the Exit door to the stairs he urged the last few of his charges towards the escape.

"Come on Alice, down the rabbit hole."

"I'm Sarah, Sir."

"How could I forget. Now get down those stairs to wonderland."

The upper flights of stairs filled with stationary bodies and he was almost the last person to get to go down a step before coming to a halt. At first he thought that the heat was from the fire, but he soon realised that it was rising from the packed exit way.

"Why are we wai-ting" he sang loudly, and there were a few sniggers from his group among the sobs and squeals.

A cool draught came up through the crowd. He guessed correctly that the people at the front had opened the outer exit doors.

John Scarings was at the front, Paula Morley beside him. He'd arrived at the bottom of the stairs to find a pair of double doors, secured by traditional old style panic bars. These bars were solid horizontal steel rods, the original fittings, mounted on pivots and levers designed to retract the vertical bolts that extended upwards and downwards into bolt holes in the frame and the floor to keep the door locked. The brilliantly simple mechanism is universally used to ensure that a packed mass of humanity's weight would open the doors without any need to turn doorknobs, simply due to pressure. The same design had kept John Mason out earlier.

The Imperial's panic bars were old with the surface rust of

decades disguised by multiple coats of paint, and needed a sharp blow to work well. However once enough bodies were behind John and Paula sheer pressure would release the locks. Both of them found this an uncomfortable experience, with the bars digging into John's stomach and Paula's chest.

The pressure grew until with a sharp metallic bang and a rattle the bars pulled from their holes and the doors opened. They lurched forward and the packed mass behind them moved too. A few inches of progress halted when the doors jammed against the solid side of Dan's truck. A welcome breath of cool wet fresh air came in. But no-one got out.

He put his shoulder against the woodwork, but John was only able to force enough gap to see, with his eye against the door, that their way was blocked by a parked van. The doors opened only about the depth of the brickwork around the door-frame. The crush was forcing the bar painfully into his midriff again.

"Back! Back! The door's blocked. We need to go back up."

But he might as well have saved his breath.. Like Canute's turning back of the tide it was a hopeless task. Even if the pupils behind had not been intent on escape by this door they could not have backed up. A few obediently turned, or at least they tried to, but the press held them where they were. Some screaming started again as those at the foot of the stairs realised the true situation, and this became communicated a little way upward.

"We're going to die! We're going to die!"

One of the pupils was overcome with such terror that they wet themselves, and a smell of urine became evident near the foot of the stairs.

And the wild wavering of light from mobile phones cast

grotesque shadows on the bare walls, tending to reinforce the impression of a dungeon, of imprisonment, of impending doom.

John knew this panic had to be stopped, but his classroom experience did not extend to what to do.

"Don't panic. It will be all right" sounded lame and feeble when the evidence so clearly contradicted what he was saying.

From below his line of sight he became conscious of a gentle tugging on his trousers. Paula had somehow wriggled down onto her knees in the scrum and was pulling at his trouser leg to attract his attention. Never had she taken independent action like this before so far as he could remember. Now, in her quiet little voice, almost inaudible to him in the racket, she said:

"I can get out."

"Don't be silly Paula."

"Sir, I can. Look!" and as she pushed her shoulder through the gap he saw that perhaps, just perhaps, at the bottom of the door where it extended below the lorry side the gap could be widened a bit to get her tiny form through.

They might save her, he thought. But what if she could take a message. He hesitated. Could Paula Morley actually manage to deliver a message? And what message? And to whom?

"Listen, Paula, if you can get out you must find someone in charge and tell them where we are. Do you understand?"

"Yes."

"Someone in uniform."

"Yes Sir."

"You've got to tell them we are trapped."

"I know."

"Tell them where we are."

"I can get out if you help push the door." Paula said, and she started to squeeze her shoulder into the gap again. John put his foot against the bottom of the door and pushed as hard as he could. The door moved slightly so the gap widened a tiny bit. The skinny girl wriggled her form into the space. Even her tiny form wedged. John could hold the pressure on the woodwork no longer. Momentarily he relaxed, the gap narrowed.

"Ow! Sir!"

"Sorry."

He redoubled his effort. Paula eased a bit more of herself out. She was backing out, her legs and one arm now in the open. She found the gap fractionally bigger at the bottom and lowered herself to the floor. With effort and with her clothes rumpled and tucked up on her she forced her hips out. Lastly she lowered her head right down to the ground and, turning it sideways managed to be free. Free, in the open air, but under a lorry. She half scrambled, half crawled across the width of the vehicle and out on the far side.

The street she emerged into was almost as dark as the stairs she had come from, but wet, and punctuated by numerous flashing blue lights instead of the wavering beams of phones. She saw no people near her, but at the top of the street a crowd lined an orange plastic barrier, guarded by police, all of whom had their backs to her,

Dan was very shocked when he finally completed his delivery. It had taken a good deal longer than he had hoped. Returning to South Parade he could hear sirens, but thought little of it. Life in the city centre rendered you immune to the two tone wail of emergency vehicles. Emerging onto the main road he found flashing blue lights and a crowd.

There were fire engines outside The Imperial now, hoses snaking in via the front doors, and police ordering people about, He hoped they were too busy to worry about his having parked down Wellington Street. Crossing the road he saw that the way to his truck was blocked by barriers. With difficulty he hauled the pallet truck into the crowd and towards the fence. He shouted to attract the attention of the nearest policeman.

"That's my truck, I need to get through."

"Stay where you are sir."

"But my son is in the truck."

"I can't help that, you can't come through."

"He's on his own, He's only four."

There was a pause while the officer digested this information.

"You've left a child unattended in a vehicle, sir?"

"I had to do a delivery," he indicated his pallet truck, "and they kept me waiting. It took longer than I thought. Just let me through and ..."

"Stay right there, sir. We'll want to have a word with you."

and the policeman started to say something into his radio.

Almost at once a police woman appeared and headed toward Dan's truck.

As she did so a small dishevelled figure crawled out from under it. Paula had got grease on her from the underside of the vehicle and her blouse had pulled out from the waistband of her skirt. She emerged a bit confused and looking about thinking she was in an empty space. Within moments the policewoman had arrived at her side and taken her hand. She led Paula to where Dan was by the fence.

"Is this your child?"

"No, no he's a little boy, he's in the cab."

"Please..." said Paula.

"I'll go and look in the cab."

"Please..." Paula tried again.

"In a minute dear. Stay here." and the policewoman made off again. She could be seen climbing up to peer through the driver's window. She didn't look downward into the foot-well.

"There's no-one there, sir." she announced when she came back.

"But there must be. He must be in there!" Dan felt a chill of panic begin. The truck had moved, he could see. Now they said his child had gone.

"Please..."

"Wait a minute, dear." The police scented a chance to issue a charge to Dan. They were unsure what, but they welcomed the opportunity with glee. The desperate pleas for attention from a small girl were of no interest by comparison.

"But they're trapped!"

"Who's trapped?" Paula's persistence finally got her a reluctant hearing.

And Paula began timidly to explain, as more and more police began to gather round her. Once her explanation was heard it wasn't many minutes before officers were around the truck trying to get in to move it clear of the exit door.

Dan's protests that he had the key were met with stern commands to stay where he was, and he was forced to watch as a policeman smashed the driver's window to open the door. The breaking glass fell on Simon and frightened him still further. The opening of the door revealed a terrified child, who was confronted, not by an angry father, as he had feared, but by a crowd of strangers in uniform. Dan's patience expired, and he leapt the barrier to run to his son. A policeman tried to grab him, but he dodged and reached the truck as Simon was being lifted out.

"Daddy. I'm sorry Daddy." Simon wept.

"It's all right son, it's all right now." Dan tried to reassure him, though the evidence of his eyes told him that it was far from 'all right'. He could see damage to the truck, and it seemed to now be jammed into a tight space. Amid the shouting, and the imperious and mostly impractical commands around the vehicle Dan now understood the problem it was causing at the exit. Heaving Simon back up into the cab he shouldered the milling police out of the way and climbed in, ignoring their orders to stop. He slammed and locked the door, brushed broken glass from the seat, and started the engine. Slowly, carefully, he backed the lorry out from the gap it had wedged into.

The moment the front cleared the exit doors they burst open under the pressure of bodies within and the mass of humanity from the stairs spilled out into the street.

Dan hesitated. His pallet truck was still on South Parade, but the police had worried him with their threatening behaviour. Gently he eased the lorry forward through the escapees, through another throng of curiously clad people by the stage door, and down Wellington Street. Those who observed him assumed that he was going to pull up further down the hill. Dan carried on, and turned out of the street, out of sight, and away into the city traffic. Just one more anonymous lorry in the early evening gloom.

"Let's go home shall we? Do your seat belt up."

Perhaps one day he would find out what Simon had done, and why. For the time being he was pleased to be away, with Simon unhurt, though he seethed at the damage.

At the lower end of Wellington Street, as Dan left it, Melvyn was walking home. Melvyn had had a bad day. Well, he considered it a bad day, though it was no worse really than any other in his life. As a photographer for the local evening newspaper he was sent, daily, to cover dull events. Today had included a one-hundreth birthday, some school children planting a tree, and a couple of local councillors opening a small shop in the suburbs. He had dutifully taken the snaps, and slavishly written down all the relevant names. Now he was going home via the newspaper office, intending to drop off the picture files and notes on the way. He could, and regularly did, send the information and the images to the paper by email from his house, but the paper was old fashioned enough to still use pigeon holes to pass messages to its staff, and he hadn't checked his for a few days. He hardly noticed Dan's truck, but he looked up the street before crossing the road, and saw the flashing of innumerable blue lights. Melvyn's day was about to become one of the highlights of his career.

He broke into a trot, camera bouncing against him on its strap. He dithered briefly as he passed the stage-door crowd, but ran on and reached the point where the exit that had been blocked was now open and free. The audience was still emerging into the open. Melvyn hoisted his camera and aimed it at the exit door. He pressed and held the shutter release at the exact moment that a half naked Gemma Barrents stumbled out, with Miss Robinson behind her with a firm hand on her shoulder. Gemma's face was streaked with tears, the effect exaggerated by the fact that she had sneaked some mascara on before the show, and it had now run. The wrist of her broken arm was now resting on a button of her blouse with her hand inside the garment. This gave support, but dragged her neckline down low. Her free hand clutched at her knickers and the lower hem of her top, trying to hide herself from view. Blood ran down her leg from the gash she had received. Melvyn's camera took a succession of photos as the flash strobed across the street at the victim.

The images would be used on front pages both locally and in the nationals tomorrow. Melvyn's career was about to receive a serious boost by the luck of being in the right place at the right time. Gemma's mother might have made objections to the pictures, were it not that while the presses were still rolling she, or rather Gemma, would be contacted by a number of photo agencies, all offering contracts for the girl. Gemma's school results were about to become unimportant, and her mother's monetary cares less vital. She might be trying to hide herself now, but soon she would be launched into a glamour model life.

His other shots by the stage door, of bedraggled cast members, including Penny in her revealing sheer wet costume, taken immediately afterwards, sold, to her chagrin, worldwide.

The tail enders escaping from the stairwell included Norah and her two new friends. Like most of the audience they stood around, unsure what to do next. Norah was unhurt, but shocked. She still leant on the arm of her new friend and thanked him again. Strangers till that moment, and thrown together only by the chance meeting in the crowd, they looked at each other.

"We should exchange phone numbers." suggested the man's wife.

But Norah was certain that this was only the woman being polite. The incident was over. She found that she was trembling with reaction, but knew it was illogical.

"Thank you." she said again, "I'm fine now."

Though the uncontrollable shivering of her body told her otherwise. She began patting her clothes down and straightening her appearance. The man and the woman drifted away into the crowd trapped against the barriers. Norah looked about.

All around her people, particularly the youngsters, were pounding their mobile phones. She thought of using hers to ring Bobby. Maybe he would see the news of the fire on TV. Maybe he would be worried. And then she decided he would still be in his shed. She was right. When she did finally get home he said:

"Did you have a nice time?"

Norah looked at her husband. She considered several responses.

"I'll start getting the supper ready." she murmured.

A realisation finally came home that after all these years she probably didn't want to tell her husband all about the trauma of the performance. She acknowledged at last that her conversations with her bed and breakfast guests were more interesting than those with her husband. Her concern for Megan and the cast members came to the fore.

Considering whether to ring Megan to check that she was all right Norah set about starting to cook the meal she had part prepared. It would take some time, and she assumed that her guests would be home earlier than usual. She could not conceive of the possibility of an evening performance that night.

Bobby, feeling that he was somehow in the wrong, but uncertain why, tried again.

"Is something the matter?" he asked cautiously.

"Why should anything be the matter."

"You seem, I don't know, upset."

"Upset! Upset, of course I'm bloody upset." she burst out, slamming a dish down with a force that threatened to destroy it, "The theatre burns down with me in it and you haven't noticed because you're in that shed pretending to mend radios, when all the while you're looking at dirty pictures, and if you'd mended just one radio you'd have heard about it on the news, and now you have to ask..." she paused, gasped a little breathlessly and then shouted, "And I don't know what's happened to those poor kids who're stopping here!" and dissolved into tears.

Bobby reached out to put his arms round her, but she shook him off angrily.

"Don't! Just find out about Megan and those boys."

He'd not been given a direct order like that in years. They had
pottered about in their own little worlds, comfortable, but
separate, now his wife had issued an instruction. Bobby
scratched his head for a moment, then put on his coat and
went out without a backward glance. Suddenly she had told
him what to do, suddenly he had a task, after years of
drifting. He had the car keys in his pocket, and was in the
city centre near the theatre not many minutes later. He was so
intent on his mission that he even failed to worry about the
discovery that she knew of his pornographic collection. He
arrived as the emergency services were clearing up. The last
ambulance had gone. Firemen were coiling hoses, fire
investigators came and went with clip-boards, and the police
barrier still closed off the road though there was little of the
crowd left. He joined what remained of it at the fence. A
young man next to him suddenly straightened and waved
down Wellington Street. Bobby followed the direction of his
attention.

The area round the stage door was fairly empty now. Cast
and crew members had made off to their digs, or in the case
of the star names had been whisked away by TV companies
for studio interviews that would be being broadcast that
evening.

Two figures were emerging from the stage door.

Within the building there had been much questioning of the
key personnel of both the "Faustus!" company and the
theatre by the fire officers, and tomorrow would bring
insurance loss adjusters and building repair men. The flames
were extinguished, even the torrent of water flooding the
basement boiler house and nearby electrics had been stopped.
Maintenance engineers of all sorts were heading towards the
stricken building. A long night of returning the venue's basic
services to working order was in prospect. Stan settled into
his stage-door keeper's hutch to observe the comings and
goings. Charlie rolled up his sleeves to start directing the

operation.

Ben had been obliged to repeat his account of what he had found on the fly-floor over and over again. Megan had had to explain her actions at the time of the disaster to the investigators. Charlie's version of events tallied so exactly that there was little to say. All parties agreed informally that everyone had done all the right things under the circumstances. The morning would see the attempts to apportion blame, and the beginnings of unfriendly legal action by solicitors seeking compensation on behalf of clients, many of whom were fabricating exaggerated trauma at that very moment, and profit for themselves.

Wearily Megan and Ben turned away from the circle of their colleagues who were speculating on the events in a pointless circular discussion that could change nothing. Like some of the audience the cast and crew were working out their shock by telling and retelling the tale of their own small part in the catastrophe. For some the effect of the incident would stay in their memories for years to come. For some the matinee of "Faustus!" would become a dinner party talking point, the spring-board for a few minutes of celebrity at any gathering.

"I was at The Imperial the night of the fire."

It would briefly raise their status from one of the crowd to that of a minor celebrity.

"Come on," Megan said now, "let's leave them to it. Tomorrow is another day."

They said goodnight to Stan as they passed his desk, and stepped out into the wet evening.

"Megan!" shouted the waving man next to Bobby.

"You know her?" he asked.

"She's my.. girlfriend." said Tom.

Bobby was not usually sensitive to inflections, but there was a momentary hesitation in the young man's statement. It registered on Bobby's blunt senses. Dimly he began to recall something Norah had told him about Megan, and her boyfriend.

Down the street he could see Megan. She looked directly toward the young man who had shouted. Then very deliberately she took the arm of the man next to her and they turned away and made off down Wellington Street.

Epilogue

At a bar counter in the city centre a man was expounding:

"...and the trouble is they've got no evacuation procedures, they just don't have them you see, no evacuation procedures... Theatres used to have them but these days...."

—

Meanwhile Sandy awoke with one of the show's tunes pounding in his head. Annoyingly there was something nearby producing a beat at the wrong tempo. Opening his eyes he could see a glaring white ceiling lit by unsympathetic fluorescent tubes. He turned his head towards the intrusive beat. The softly bleeping monitor was beside the bed.

"Hello," said the nurse, "you're back with us again. That's good."

In a nearby out-patients ward Miss Robinson scowled at Gemma's mother across the girl's bed and made preparations for leaving. She bristled with annoyance that this awful trip should have resulted in promoting this little tart into a modelling career.

—

John gave her a lift home. They stood awkwardly outside her front door, then abruptly Patsy turned and fumbled with the lock.

"Will you come in for a coffee?" she asked shyly.

—

"Norah's going to be very upset when I fetch my things tomorrow." said Megan, "She wasn't best pleased when I told her on the phone that I wouldn't be back for supper tonight."

Ben nodded tiredly and shifted his arm slightly.

"Oh sorry," she said, "am I squashing you?"

"It's all right. But I think I'd better get a double bed."

"I think we'd better get a quieter flat." Megan told him, as a neighbouring student scrolled down the play-list on their ipod, loudly skipping from track to track.

It was the early hours of the morning.

At about the same time an unremarkable and somewhat battered truck pulled quietly to a stop opposite The Imperial.

The barriers had been shoved back to the theatre's frontage, so, although the pavement outside the old building was blocked, traffic was flowing along South Parade again.

A figure jumped from the van, ran to the back and lowered the tailgate lift. He collected a hand operated pallet truck from the pavement near an alley-way and loaded it into the vehicle.

Moments later, with the back of the truck shut, he got back into the cab and drove gently away, back home, where his small child was sleeping.